CW00868354

NORTH OF

MIDNIGHT

BY THE SAME AUTHOR

A Clash of Ichor and Blood

Writing as Mark P. Lynch

Hour of the Black Wolf

No Fire Without Smoke

NORTH OF
MIDNIGHT

short stories

Mark Patrick Lynch

RAGSTONE HOLLOW PRESS

NORTH OF MIDNIGHT

First published in paperback by Ragstone Hollow Press
2018

Copyright Mark Patrick Lynch 2018

Mark Patrick Lynch asserts the moral right to
be identified as the author of this work.

This book is entirely a work of fiction. The names,
characters and incidents portrayed within these pages
are entirely the work of the author's imagination. Any
resemblance to actual persons, living or dead, events
and localities, is entirely coincidental.

ISBN-13: 978-1727150117
ISBN-10: 1727150112
e-book available

Set in Garamond

All rights reserved. No part of this publication may be
reproduced,
stored in a retrieval system, or transmitted in any form or by
any means - electronic, mechanical, photocopying,
recording, or otherwise - without the prior permission of the
author and the publishers.

CONTACT:
twitter: @markplynch
markpatricklynch.blogspot.com

NORTH OF
MIDNIGHT

Contents

the light of
a shadow

Every so often, when the moons of Jupiter are in alignment or one of the prophecies of Nostradamus comes up in the news, my next door neighbour Noah Williams tries his luck and knocks on my door to invite me out on a date.

Noah's a cute enough guy in a nouveau-geek kind of way, and I know plenty of girls who'd like to be seen on his arm. But I'm never entirely sure about his priorities. And that matters to me. I'm the sort of person who likes to know which way a man's facing on a subject before I commit too deeply. It's one of my hang-ups. Noah changes direction like a newspaper caught in a hurricane and therefore is *not* someone I could be comfortable with. One day he's walking around with a placard supporting striking workers, the next he's calling on the government to legislate against trade unions. But he is persistent when he's running to a personal agenda, I'll give him that.

When I opened my door and saw him standing

outside my apartment, hair typically and nicely awry, a bunch of yellow flowers in his hand, I assumed he'd heard that I'd broken up with Christopher, the guy I'd been seeing semi-regularly for the last year, and he'd decided to make another play for me.

"No, Noah. Let me stop you before you begin. Thanks for the thought. You're a great guy, I've told you that enough. But honey, you and me – we're talking alternative universes."

Noah didn't drop his sad smile but his shoulders did slump fractionally.

"You know, that's one thing I've always liked about you, Gretchen. You don't waste time letting a guy know his place. Even when he's standing somewhere else."

My face must've been all hanging jaw – "Huh?" – because he explained politely but as if to an imbecile,

"I'm not here to ask you out."

"You're not?"

"Don't be too offended, okay." He pulled at the knot on his loose tie. It was strange seeing him dressed up. Noah hardly ever wears a suit. I've heard him say they're too restricting and I can't remember the last time I saw him in one, even though we've shared the same building for years and bump into each other almost daily. "But honestly," he said, "just this once, this isn't about you."

"Then why're you here?"

"Advice?"

I thought about it a moment, wondering if this was some new bug-out idea he'd come up with to blindside me and try persuade me to go for a drink with him after all. Noah works in computer gaming and strategies come easily to him. But he looked sincere, and as I've already said, kinda cute in his lost geek way.

"Sure, that's fine," I said. "I can do advice."

A few minutes later we were nursing black coffees at different ends of the sofa. I'd put the flowers in a vase, even though they weren't for me. They stood before us on the low coffee table that's really just a sheet of bevelled glass on corner legs made from stacked hardcover art books, mainly ones that I've reviewed over the years.

Noah indicated his tie and good jacket as I curled my legs up between us.

"I had some legal stuff to sort out today, hence the suit. When I came out of the offices, Bella gave those to me." He stared at the yellow flowers but seemed to find something about their shape and texture he didn't like. His lip curled. "No one's ever given me flowers before. I wasn't sure what to do with them. I should probably just throw them away."

"Okay, you're gonna have to back up a little. Bella is ... ?"

He sighed, took his eyes off the flowers and focused on me. "Do you ever get the feeling that the one person you've been searching for all your life, your soul-mate, I guess you'd call them . . . do you ever get the feeling that you've maybe already met them but somehow never realised it?"

"Only in nightmares." I squeezed the cushion I found myself hugging. "You think this Bella is ... ?"

"No. I don't. I really don't. But she thinks I'm hers."

"Ah."

"Yeah – big ah. And it gets worse."

I wondered how.

"There's this guy, see. He's really into her, doesn't like anyone else . . . uh . . ." Noah floundered. "I don't know how you'd put it."

"Vying for her affection."

"Something like that."

"But you're not. Unless I've misread this? No? I didn't think so. Then have you talked to him? Told him you're not looking for a relationship with her?"

"He's not the talking to kind of guy." He pushed a finger to squish his nose over, making his profile look like that of a villain from central casting.

"Shit. You think he's going to come after you, do something to hurt you?"

He shrugged helplessly. "Maybe."

Poor guy, he looked so dejected. Noah would fight a hundred battles for you on a computer screen, but he's never going to be anyone's idea of a knight of yore, ready to do battle with a real life sword and shield. I didn't know what to say, whether I should slink across the suede cover of the sofa to hug him or not. In the end I didn't do either of those things and instead lifted my mug to my lips and took a sip of coffee.

"I really don't know what to do about this, Gretchen."

"Look, if you can't talk to this guy, you need to

find a way of telling this Bella that you don't have the same feelings for her that she has for you. You're not interested in her. And if she goes away and leaves you alone, her jealous would-be boyfriend's got nothing on you. Right?"

It sounded like good advice to me and would probably have looked okay in a readers' advice column in a trashy magazine. But we were talking real world here and Noah wasn't so easily fooled.

"So I just tell her and it's as easy as that? Like you tell me you're not interested, and I never ask you to see a movie with me ever again?"

I had the grace to look mildly embarrassed while still getting the point across to him that, yes, that's exactly what I meant.

He waved his arms about in frustration. "I've tried. Honestly, I have. But . . . She's kind of . . . Oh God, this sounds so melodramatic. But Gretchen, I swear, I think the woman's stalking me. She's everywhere I go. Either just arriving as I'm leaving a place, or else just coming out as I walk in. Making a point of it, too, so that I see her. And now she's giving me presents."

We both stared at the dainty yellow flowers.

"Kinda hard to tell the police there's a woman being evil to you by giving you presents, isn't it?"

I was trying to be funny, but Noah's head fell when I mentioned the police. When he looked up his eyes were glistening, ready to shed tears. His pleasing face crumpled. "Jesus, Gretch. This is serious, isn't it?"

"I think you need to tell me more. How often does she turn up, day to day? What else has she given you?"

He let me know, and it was worse than I'd imagined. This girl must do nothing but follow Noah around all of her day; she had to be camping outside his door, watching his windows while he slept. A squadron of secret service agents couldn't know more about his movements than this misguided creature did. She was taking over his every waking moment and it had gotten so that it was eating into him while he dreamed.

"I can't believe I've never noticed her," I told him when he'd done. I eyed the flowers warily now, as if they contained a surprise venus fly trap or a bomb. "Someone spends so long following you, then I should've seen her."

"You probably have. But she doesn't really stand out much." He described her, an average sized dark-haired girl with passing to fair looks that you enjoyed and forgot about straight away. Like a hundred thousand other girls in the city. She didn't dress provocatively, had a simple haircut, wasn't loud. Who were you gonna call about her, what were you gonna say? No one and nothing. She just is. Like newspaper street vendors, the cat slinking along the sidewalk, and the weather forecast on your cell phone.

"The guy, then. The boyfriend. What about him? How bad is he, really? Can't we get him to take her off our hands, make it seem like we're on his side?"

Noah smiled. Genuine warmth lighted his face for the first time since he'd slumped onto the sofa. "Thanks."

"Why? For what?"

"For saying 'our' just then and not 'your'."

"It wasn't a conscious thing," I told him perfectly honestly.

He reached across, covered his hand over mine for a second. I was still hugging the cushion. "Then it's even kinder of you. But there's no way I'm approaching the guy. He makes mountains look small."

I shook my head. "Okay, so the boyfriend's out. We still need to figure out what to do, though. Maybe together we'll get there. I know that you won't want to get the police involved, but I know a way to a guy on the local squad. He's a friend's boyfriend. Maybe I could talk to her and get him to do something."

Noah gave a low moan. For a moment I thought he was going to sink his head into his hands. He looked so lost. "Do we have to get official about this?"

"You know we do. Even if it's just to put a marker down in case anything more serious happens."

"Gretch. This is making it seem awfully real and ugly."

"Noah, if you're telling me the truth, this woman's taking over your life!"

"I know, but . . ."

"But what? There can be no 'buts' about this. Seriously. Something has to be done. We can't just sit back and let her plague you this way. How long's it going to be until she starts making a mess of things for you? Oh, I don't know how – maybe stealing your mail, running up a credit account in your name, or pretending to be people on the phone so she can get close to you. This kind of craziness does happen."

He sank back into the sofa, defeated.

I tried to sound sure about this. "I'll talk to my friend Sally, see if her cop can do anything for us. Until then, hold tight, okay."

He mimed gripping onto empty air, made the corners of his lips turn up into a facsimilie of happiness. But it was an empty gesture on both counts. He looked ready to fall right back down when he stood up and his smile wasn't fooling anyone. When he left my apartment, I gave him a quick kiss on the cheek. After he'd gone I took the vase to the trash can and then, not satisfied with that, changed my mind and went out and dropped the whole sorry lot in the dumpster out back. It'd begun to rain and I hurried back inside, catching the communal door to the lobby before it closed. Someone had just left. I'd gone by her before I'd noticed. When I glanced back she wasn't there. Cautiously, as if measuring the wind, I stood searching for any sign of her. But it was as if she was invisible. Even the scent of her perfume had thinned to nothing.

An ordinary-sized dark-haired girl, Noah had said. Forget her as soon as you've seen her.

I shook my head and went back upstairs.

That night I called Sally and told her the situation. She promised to speak to her boy in blue about it.

But the next morning, before I was even out the building for work, Noah was at my door. He was looking . . . I can only call it "abashed", the way he hung his head, so that his hair fell across his face in wavy tresses. He reminded me of a teenager sent by his mom to apologise for a stupid misdemeanour he'd committed.

"What is it?" I already knew I wouldn't like what he'd have to say.

He continued to stare at the floor. "You didn't, uh, you know, call your buddy, did you? The one who knows the cop?"

"Noah . . ."

"See, I was hoping you hadn't, because, like, well . . ."

"Noah, please. Stand up straight. Look at me when you're talking to me at least." I reached for his chin before he could pull away and lifted his face up. "Oh my God!"

"It's only a bruise," he said, quickly hiding the wreckage of his face and talking to the floor again. "It'll fade."

"Noah, who did that, it's terrible. Was it the boyfriend? Was it Bella's boyfriend? Tell me, honey, you have to tell me. You can't let something like that go. Let me see."

"It's nothing."

But it wasn't. The whole left side of his face was a welter of bruising. Angry yellows and horrific blacks. As if someone had tried to pull his forehead down to his jaw. One of his eyes had swollen so much that he couldn't have been able to see out of it clearly.

"I'm just here to apologise, Gretchen. I'm sorry I got you involved. I shouldn't have gotten you into this. That was my mistake. I'm sorry. And I'm so sorry about your door. I'll send someone over to fix it up for you."

"My door? What's wrong with my . . . ? Oh shit."

"It's only graffiti. It'll come off."

"Jesus. The bitch did this, didn't she? She watched you come around here and saw me dump the flowers. Is she watching us now? Did she send you?" I peered down the corridor both ways but there was no one to see.

"I gotta go, Gretchen. Like I said, I'm sorry for everything. And I'll get that door fixed for you, I promise. Just – please, you know, make the stuff with the cop go away. It's for the best. I'm okay. You're okay. Bella's okay."

"You've seen her? Did you speak to her?"

"Gretchen . . ."

"Noah."

He mumbled, "It's all okay. It's settled."

Then he was gone, leaving me to stand open-mouthed as I watched him leave. When he'd disappeared down the stairs, I read the abuse scrawled on my door. That alone was enough to leave me fuming. Even when it was sanded down and painted over, I knew those hurtful words would still be there, waiting for me in the back of my mind every time I came home. This Bella was a piece of work, all right. I phoned Sally right away, told her what had happened. Her cop bf was there with her and I spoke to him.

"Truth of it is there's nothing we can do unless you witnessed this woman marking your door," he told me. "You didn't, did you?"

Of course I hadn't. Who sits up all night guarding

the paint on their apartment door?

With Noah unwilling to take things further Sally's guy advised me that any official investigation was going to fall flat on its ass before it even stood up. I thanked him, talked to Sally some more, hung up, and headed off to work a half hour late.

The days passed. I didn't see Noah for some time. Whenever I went by his apartment the door was always shut and there were rarely any lights shining out of his windows at night. Even the flicker of his TV was absent. But when you live in the same building it's impossible to avoid someone for ever. One day, a couple of months after he'd knocked on my door and asked for my advice about Bella, I came home early from work, and almost walked into him as he was leaving the building. There was no sign of the damage that had been inflicted to his face when I'd spoken to him last, and he wasn't alone.

"Oh. Hi Gretch," he said, sounding really pleased to see me.

"Noah."

I was eyeing the girl on his arm. Was this the creature that had vandalised my door? She clung to him as if she were afraid she'd disappear if she let go. Dark-haired, conservatively dressed, with nothing showy enough to stand out. Even now the shadows seemed to pull at her edges, making them blur. But there were thick clouds today and the light had gone in the lobby. It could be an explanation. Everything was slightly dull.

"We were just leaving," Noah said, smiling at me.

"But it's really great seeing you. It's been weeks. Of course, I've hardly been here and all . . . Still. You know."

"Sure," I told him. Why was he so happy?

"This is Bella," he said, seeing that I was waiting for more. "We're moving in together. I've been staying over with her. We've just come here to parcel some things up. I've a removals van coming at the weekend."

I met Bella's eyes. She seemed like such a fragile creature, one of those small mammals that hides in a burrow and lives a life of perpetual fright and scurrying flight. I couldn't imagine her having enough heat in her to melt sugar in her mouth, let alone ruin my door. I wondered what had happened to the jealous boyfriend, and how or even *if* any of that had been resolved. But it was Noah I was more interested in. There was no artifice to him, there rarely had been, and he was being genuine now, too. He clearly wasn't scared of the boyfriend. I could feel the enthusiasm for this new life on which he was embarking fizz around him like static electricity.

How to explain that? I'm not sure I can. Maybe something about Bella had finally adhered to him after she'd told him he was her soul mate and seemingly struck out. Or maybe it was simply another example of Noah blowing one way on Monday and then flitting out of there in a completely new direction come Tuesday. Who can honestly say?

"Well, I hope you'll both be happy," I said and stepped out of their way, because that's all I could think to do.

They went. The dark-haired girl clung to Noah all the way, as if afraid he might run away from her. As I watched them walk along the sidewalk I found it hard to tell where each of them started and ended, because they seemed to blur into one creature, eating each other up. I stayed there, watching, until eventually they faded from sight altogether and were gone.

Unsettled, but not entirely sure as to the reasons why, I turned around and went inside, being sure to close the door behind me.

what i
wouldn't give

When I first set eyes on Chrissie Rhodes, I thought she was the kind of girl who could make the heavens sing.

She was a piece of work, all right, with strong blue eyes, soft yellow hair, straight white teeth, and one of those tanned complexions you see airbrushed to perfection on the covers of supermarket magazines.

Standing under a long, green awning outside an expensive hotel in the middle of the city of York, she'd ducked out of the rain just as the pavements began to stain and people vanished into the stores for cover. Ancient architecture darkened around her and the past whirled about on leathery wings. It was the kind of shot you'd expect to see at the beginning of a romantic movie.

A stray sail of sunlight lit her amidst the old stonework and I didn't think twice about pulling over into the lay-by and stopping, even though I'd pay hell trying to get back into traffic. It was all instinct on my part, even then. Acting without thinking. Being lured on by some desire I wasn't prepared to admit to.

As soon as it arrived, the sunlight passed over her, leaving her suddenly small and lost, and the deluge began. Thick heavy rain accompanied by rumblings of thunder.

She glanced at the lettering on the side of the cab and came out from under her shelter. She held a large leather handbag over her head in an attempt to avoid getting too badly soaked and walked in small but confident steps, her legs cutting across the pavement quickly like scissors. With her other hand she carried a thin rectangular item that might have been an art folder. It was in a thick-skinned, white plastic bag lacking store decals, and it whipped and turned in the rain, pushing against her legs as if to trip her like a disobedient child.

Chrissie headed toward the back of the car. I leaned over the seat and pushed the rear door open, wondering why I was doing this and if it was worth the risk. I'm licensed for private hire only, pre-booked fares. Shouldn't pick up off the street; it's illegal. But something called me to her. Maybe it was because of the rain, how vulnerable she looked under the awning while people fled indoors. Or else it was that bright fan of light setting her out from the crowd. Technicolor lady in a world of noir extras.

Whatever. I stopped. I let her in. My choice.

She pulled the door wide, and the noise of the rain increased for a moment as she slipped inside and smiled at me. The car warmed and filled with her scent as soon as she shut out the Gene Kelly backing track. The atmosphere inside the cab drew close and intimate. When she spoke, it was on the back of a heavy breath, and it wasn't hard to imagine her beating breast beneath the palm of a lover's hand.

"Thanks for stopping. How'd you know I needed a cab?"

"Everyone needs a cab sometimes. I just saw you and thought it was your day for one. I'm Matt." I pointed to my licence on the dashboard, the one I have next to Sonny's picture and the details for the appeal. If she took it in, she didn't show it.

"Okay, well, score one for you, Matt. You're just what I need. Chrissie Rhodes – pleased to meet you."

Her accent was mid-Atlantic nowhere. She shuffled across the rear seat until she was comfortably settled with all her gear and then pulled on the belt, clicking the metal clasp into the plastic. She tossed her hair back in the way only beautiful women can do without making it a performance, and brushed her fingers through the waves, patting everything back into place.

I could smell her: the light kisses of the rain and her perfume mixing like scented water, something warm and spicy, sensually exotic. I couldn't help but think how the seat would feel after she'd gone, the heat her presence would leave.

Dangerous thoughts. Very dangerous. So keep your head on the job, turn your eyes to the road, driver.

"Gonna tell me where we're going?"

She gave me an address outside the city walls, toward the racecourse, and I indicated to pull out, knowing that so late in the day we'd find it hard to slot back into the traffic. The windscreen wipers sounded out of time with the ticking of the blinkers, grinding unpleasantly, and because I figured we'd be here a while I shut them off, letting the rain-snakes slide over the screen and make blurs of York and the few people still left on the streets.

With the wipers silent the car felt even more self-contained than usual. The rain rattled on the roof as if we were inside a bunker. Our breathing seamed louder somehow. Chrissie's clothes, wet in just the short distance between the hotel and the car, steamed up the back of the cab as she dried out. I flicked on the rear screen heater and sneaked a look in the mirror, taking in more of my new fare as she settled down.

She was wearing a raincoat a size too large. It had been belted around her waist in a loose, tied-together style that spoke casual but also somehow managed to say that the way she looked was more important than dressing to keep out the cold. It wasn't done up and was slumping open now as she sat, letting you see a white woman's shirt, probably silk, unbuttoned enough to show the swell of tanned cleavage below a couple of thin gold necklaces. Her trousers were expensive and Italian, cut short, flashing her perfect calves as she crossed her legs. Her light heels were fastened with gold gossamer.

Not wet weather wear at all.

Standing under the awning as she had been, there was almost no chance of her scoring a passing cab, no matter how good looking she was. With traffic like this, you had to go to the edge of the road, even when there was somewhere easy to pull in like this lay-by. It gave the driver the option of choosing to ignore the lay-by if he wanted and block the other cars, making it easier to get going again. Do that or you'd be standing waiting all day. Okay, I'd been seduced by her and taken pity, pulled in. But that kind of thing wouldn't always happen. I decided to tell her as much, a little advice from someone who knows.

"I can give you a tip if you like, Chrissie."

"Isn't it usually the other way around?"

"Sorry?"

"Aren't I supposed to give you the tip when we stop?"

I laughed. "Sure, if you like. But it's not compulsory. I'm used to business accounts these days, everything paid for later. I hardly do the pick-ups any more. How about you?" I gave her the once-over in the mirror, making sure she could see me do it this time. "I'd say you're in business."

"I sell things."

"You do? Anything I'd know about?"

"Perhaps. What's your tip?"

I didn't get a chance to tell her because right then a horn beeped, and looking over my shoulder I saw a big car, a Lexus or Beemer, hard to be sure of which in the rain, flashing its headlights at me to come out into the road. That was a wonder in itself, because the rule generally tends to be that the bigger the car the less likely the driver is to let you out. I've driven professionally for fifteen years and the least polite people on the roads are the ones with the nicest cars. Next time you're driving, check to see who brakes to let you join the throng. I guarantee nine times out of ten it won't be the suit in the sparkling new Mercedes.

Not one to throw away a break like this, I shuttled into gear and pulled out. "All right," I said. "Here we go."

We squeezed onto the road and I started the wipers going again, watching the primary coloured blurs of people in macs and rain-hats resolve into focus as they scurried by us. I killed any chance the windows had of fogging up by putting on the blowers and buzzing my side window open a crack, tried to settle into the awkward sound of the grind of the blades swishing the windscreen. The wipers probably needed replacing, another expense to add to the tally come the next service.

I didn't say anything to Chrissie as I concentrated on the stop/start queue ahead of us. When we were stuck at the lights leading around the ring road toward the Micklegate Bar I remembered I hadn't given Chrissie her tip. I looked in the rear-view about to speak, but paused when I noticed she was fishing in her purse for something.

Okay, I know I shouldn't have kept looking, should have turned my eyes back on the road. Give the fare his or her privacy is the rule. But she was eager for whatever she was searching for in her bag and I couldn't help noticing she had the longest fingers I've ever seen on a woman. Surprisingly long, much longer than my own, with pointed red nails. I had one of those moments when you realise that even the most attractive people also have flaws. Her fingers were the length of a basketball player's, though soft and velvety to the touch, no doubt. That her palms were ordinary sized only made the fingers appear even more elongated. I thought of that advert that'd been on TV so often when I was a kid, soft on your hands washing cleaner – "with mild green Fairy Liquid." I seemed to remember the woman in that had long fingers, too.

Chrissie produced a little foldout wallet from her bag, the kind you'd use for keeping identity and store cards in, and it set me wondering about what kind of sales she was involved in. I'd hardly marked her down as a door-to-door; I couldn't imagine her bothering old ladies for the sake of a new vacuum cleaner or a monthly supply of make-up. *Hi, my name's Chrissie – how would you like a set of Everyman Bibles?*

If someone like Chrissie says she's in sales you've got to be looking at designer wear, or property . . . maybe those big ivy-clad houses in their own grounds, which you see when you're heading out north toward the national park. She's not gonna be selling a clip-together photo-frame with a slightly out-of-focus aerial view of your house.

I was staring and knew it. Chrissie caught me looking at her in the mirror and straightaway I did eyes forward, breaking contact and feeling guilty because I didn't want her to think I was spying.

Just drive, that's the job; the rest's incidental. People catching you doing a surveillance job in the rear-view is not on any of the cabbies' recommended lists. I guess that because I wasn't used to someone being in the back, the way of an old style pick-up fare, I was feeling edgy about not being able to see her directly, and had been suckered into staring by her fingers and wondering what she was going to produce from her wallet. Now it felt like I'd been caught sneaking a glance at Chrissie herself, intruding on her privacy . . . which I guess is precisely what I had been doing.

I put my efforts into nudging the car through the busy street, tightened my grip on the steering wheel.

After a while the back of my neck began to itch. I concentrated on the road and did my best to ignore the feeling, telling myself I was imagining it as we crawled through traffic and the day edged slowly on. I was getting hotter. Sweat broke out and slunk down my spine.

When I thought a safe few minutes had passed I looked again, intending a quick glance, perhaps accompanied by my best winning smile, hoping she'd gone back to her purse or was into whatever she wanted from the little wallet. But when I checked in the rear-view I found myself looking straight into her eyes.

I knew then. She hadn't taken her stare off me the whole time I was driving us out past the walls and Micklegate Bar. My itching neck and rising temperature told me so; it was something like instinct, the primitive part of ourselves we forget still exists but which is always ready to sense the threat of the leopard in the night.

Feeling I had to say something, and pretty sure my

winning smile would fail if I tried that, I came out with a lame, "Look, I'm sorry I was watching you back then. I didn't mean to . . ."

But her face tuned in an expression I didn't want to think about, one of those *beyond* fierce affairs, and I couldn't find another thing to say.

"Shut up. Just drive. Do your job."

She spoke – *snarled,* if you want to get melodramatic – in such a way that I knew it was pointless to do anything but as she commanded. Apologies wouldn't work here. I was familiar enough with the score: it was her ride, her decision as to whether we talked or not; and although if I had a choice I preferred polite, I could handle quiet and uncomfortable, too.

I drove Chrissie the rest of the way in silence, keeping my eyes off the rear-view as much as I could, relying on the wing mirrors instead. Every so often I glanced at the picture of Sonny on the passenger side of the dashboard to keep things straight.

Take a look at him and the whole world gets put into perspective. So I had a top-of-the-range bitch with an anger management problem in the back of the cab. Big deal. She'd get out eventually; I'd go home and then ready the car for an overnight to the airport. End of.

I speculated about my passenger as I drove, though. The best I could come up with was that maybe Chrissie Rhodes was an addict, needed a little hit before she got to wherever she had to be and that was why she was pissed off that I might have seen some personal item or other in her handbag. She might be worried I'd caught a glimpse of her shooting up equipment: her hypodermic, her mirror and razorblade or whatever it is these people use. It would be something along those lines. There's nearly always a reason why people get cranked.

But I couldn't see nerves being an issue for her when we did get to her destination. It wasn't the kind of place where you'd expect her to be uncomfortable, not a woman looking like she did.

We were in the area to which she'd directed me, but I didn't know where Chrissie wanted to stop. As I was working up the courage to ask, she spoke and gave me her instructions. "Take a left here, then up ahead you hang a right by the blue car, and stop just before the next turn-off."

It wasn't what I was expecting as an endpoint, but I pulled over and gave her a price, which she paid without blinking. No tip, which served me right for offering her one earlier, I guessed. Just the asking price; a deal done with no comebacks, service rendered paid for. Transactions honoured.

She was still angry with me. But she treated me with the kind of studied indifference that suggests a person has been wiped clean off the slate of existence. For all she cared I was no longer of this earth. She handed me some money without speaking and got out of the cab and back into the rain, pulling her big flapping holder and her handbag with her. The door shut without a goodbye from her.

I sat for a while as I watched her cut her fast walk

up the path to an ordinary enough suburban row house, maybe a bit more rundown than the others in the terrace, door in need of a lick of paint, windows still wooden framed, garden bleak and forgotten. Not once did she look back to check on me. She examined the front door and then knocked after dismissing the electric buzzer. A slight nervy woman who reminded me of a mouse, timid and huddled up against the world, answered.

Chrissie walked straight in without waiting for permission, forcing the little woman to move aside before she was ploughed over. When her visitor was inside the woman glanced out onto the street, looking glad of the rain . . . The way she did it, with more than just a hint of the furtive about it, you'd almost think she was worried Chrissie had been seen going into her house. When she saw me parked at the kerb, the wipers cutting a clear arc across the windscreen, she froze as if she'd been caught committing a crime.

What *was* Chrissie selling?

The mouse woman pulled back into the house and shut the door. I waited a moment to see if anything else was going to happen and then when it didn't (unless you count the flickering blue glow of the TV being switched off in what I guessed was the living room) I put the car into gear and pulled away.

Tell the truth, I was still surprised I'd stopped for Chrissie in the first place. It wasn't entirely out of character with the person I'd been ten or fifteen years ago, but I hadn't even thought about doing anything like that in at least a half decade. I thought again that it must've been the way she'd been standing under the hotel awning, rain bouncing around her, the light hitting her – she'd looked like a movie star. I think I might have needed the prospect of something like that walking into my life just then.

A little bit of magic. The prospect of some kind of hope.

When I got home and pulled the car into the garage I did my usual job of cleaning out the back seat and vacuuming the floor mats. The business card I found was expensive and none too flexible; speckled white dots on delicately hued veins that looked like a geology lesson. It was superimposed with embossed gold lettering in a script.

Chrissie Rhodes

There was a stylised silhouette of a woman's profile beside it. My snarling customer from today, the romantic movie heroine with the temper. The shape of the nose and little oxbow lips gave her away. If her hair had been dry and not wet as it had been in the cab, it would've looked the way it did in the logo – waved and styled like any of the three girls in the opening credits of the 70's version of *Charlie's Angels*.

There was no contact number and no address, just her name. I turned the card over a few times, and even put it up to my nose. It had no scent but felt cold, made me think of the kind of thing Japanese businessmen present to you with two hands and their heads bowed.

Well, what about you, I thought.

A card as expensive as this – it felt like it might be made out of some form of rock, sliced and then polished – would certainly be missed. I'd heard of them before, even been shown a few in my time, though of course never actually been in receipt of one. It put a whole new perspective on my ride with Chrissie, bumped her up the importance scale a few notches. But why had she been looking to hail a cab when she should've had a limousine waiting for her?

Impossible to say really. And given my experience today, any thoughts about her still came down to an indifferent, *So what?*

So she was some stuck-up business type earning even more than I'd first thought . . . possibly dogged with a habit, too. What did I care? It wasn't like I'd be bumping into her again. The chances of her needing a cab in the first place must have been so astronomically high that there wasn't enough room for all the zeros on the screen of a calculator, and the likelihood of my being there for her not once but twice would be even greater. Especially as I never pulled over for strangers any more. Except I had done today, hadn't I?

I kept hold of the card, showed it to Bobbi my wife, and told her about Chrissie.

"Matt, you stopped for someone? What were you thinking?"

Which wasn't a reaction I could blame her for having. We were paying close to four grand a year in insurance to trade as a private hire firm and picking up non-booked rides would invalidate my policy; also, we could wind up with a hefty fine if we were caught. But as I told her more about her, my passenger intrigued Bobbi, too.

"Did she say what she sells?"

I shook my head and picked up a cloth to dry some of the dishes Bobbi was stacking after washing them in the sink – with mild green Fairy Liquid, wouldn't you know?

"No, but it must be some direct to home sales pitch she does."

"Maybe she's in insurance."

I could see that. To some degree. It would account for the big folder she was carrying in the plastic bag. But it was still speculation. She could be almost anything. Maybe it was a kitchen design she'd taken to show the mousy woman. Chrissie Rhodes, kitchen designer to the slightly unkempt suburbs. It was kind of funny to picture. But it didn't explain the expensive card. Or why the mouse woman had looked so anxious when she realised that I'd seen Chrissie enter her home.

Heading back to the garage, where the office and computer are, I put the card in my spiffy little M.B.J. Cabs roller holder. (Yeah, we've got all the gear.) I didn't need to call her, and anyway there wasn't any contact information on it even if I had wanted to; the card was just something of a talking point. I imagined getting it out once in a while, holding it between two fingers like a playing card you're about to trump someone with. *Ever seen a business card made out of stone? Well, here, take a look at this.*

I finished cleaning the car and quietly went about forgetting Chrissie Rhodes. I did what everyone does and got on with my life.

After the car's cleaned the next thing on the itinerary – the most important thing on the itinerary – is Sonny. He's a fighter, my kid. Gonna knock all the girls dead when he grows up. A looker just like his mother, he's eight years old right now, and small for his age, but he's got the biggest blue eyes you've ever seen, long golden hair with flowing waves that make you think he should be in a shampoo ad, and a smile as wide as summer.

Thing is, there's a problem.

The doctors say that he's going to die before he makes his way very far into his teens. It's one of those diseases you only hear about if someone you know has it; and even then you'll take a few turns at learning to pronounce it, let alone figure out how you spell it. There's a website (isn't there always?), and about fifteen other kids in the world have it at any one time. And it is, in theory, damn near curable.

The only catch comes down to the question of who's going to put forty or fifty million pounds into finding a fix for something that only a couple of kids die of each year.

Most evenings, after all the fares have been routed, and unless I've an overnight run, I spend time searching the web, hunting the email addresses of the best doctors in the world and mailing them with the information about Sonny's disease. Long flickering nights of uncertainty pass as I wait for the inbox to light up with a message from some apologetic doctor in California, say, telling me he sympathises and wishes us all, Sonny included, the best of luck in finding a cure, which he's sure is out there somewhere. But sorry, he can't help right now.

Sometimes there'll be new contact numbers and addresses with the mail – more often not.

Is it depressing?

No.

Yes.

No.

I don't know.

Maybe it's the trying that's important. If I just sat brooding then I'd go crazy. And who knows? Maybe I am a little crazy; maybe we both are, Bobbi and me. She won't talk about it much. If I mention the Internet and doctors she just looks away and turns off. It's like a switch has been thrown somewhere inside her head. She acts as if we've never spoken about Sonny's illness . . . Like the blind spot in an eye, she just looks around what she can't see. We all have our different ways to cope.

A few local businesses that use the cab company regularly helped with fundraising appeals for research once we found out Sonny was ill and we first got the diagnosis. They even helped get me on the local TV news a couple of times. I've found that business people are good individuals on the whole; it's only when you deal with them piecemeal that you get the nasties, those who dehumanise themselves to score a little more profit, and even then they're few and far between. Tough guys in the boardroom you'd expect, but by themselves, mostly they have heart. Now any money we get in goes on campaigns. Just a few of us scattered around the world trying to nudge the seemingly unmovable course of multinationals involved in medical research. You'd have more luck getting a seahorse to change the direction of an oil tanker. But you've got to try. If you didn't, you'd just go insane.

I forgot about Chrissie's card once it was in the roller holder and shut down the office. A fare to Manchester airport from Thirsk at two tomorrow morning and that was it till noon. I could turn on the PC and check my mail, but I decided to wait till after I'd popped upstairs to see how my boy was doing.

He was in his room playing a video game. I watched from the open door a while. Little electronic blips were being fired from his quick fingers on the joypad. X-Box or Playstation, I can't remember which it is. Machines like that are a couple of light years away from the toys of my youth; I'm old enough to have been among the last wave of kids who had board games and Airfix kits; Spitfires dangling from my ceiling on fishing-wire strafing German bombers . . . Now, I saw a whole future in my boy's reflecting eyes, and I thought about how far toys would have moved on by the time he got to my age.

If he got to my age.

Because that's the punch-line every time: everything's an if. *If* he makes next year's birthday. *If* this Christmas is going to be our last. *If* the Father's Day cards stop coming. That's another thing. They all mean so much more now, the cards: Father's Day, birthday, Christmas. It's even got so we give each other Easter Cards, something we'd never have done if Sonny hadn't been ill. This year Sonny bought Bobbi a Valentine's Card. She opened it quietly, with tears tricking the blue of her eyes brighter. I know she has it still, packed away under the bed in a small loose drawer that came from an old furniture set we don't have any more. Sonny posted it through the front door with a hand-drawn stamp. When Bobbi asked why he'd sent it, he said it was because he wanted to have sent at least one in his life.

My boy . . .

Oh God.

But you take what you can.

"Hiya, Sonny."

"Hey, Dad."

"New game?" I pushed myself off the doorframe and sauntered into his room.

"It's one of Pete's – he lent it me."

"I like Pete. He's a good guy." I hunkered down next to him, sat cross-legged on the floor, watched more bug-eyed aliens turn to green pixel goo on the screen. Sonny has framed emails on his walls, sent by some of his heroes that he's contacted over the net. There're signed photographs of footballers and children's writers, TV stars and minor pop singers. Cuddly animals lay scattered around the floor like a suicide bomber ran into a Disney store and pulled the detonator cord, each brightly grinning for a hug. "When did you see Pete?"

"Called around last night when you were taking that guy and his wife to the Oprah."

"The opera."

"Yeah." Big smile and a glance from the screen at me and then back. "I know. But Pete calls it the *Oprah* – like that American woman on the television, the one who does the show where everyone hugs each other and cries."

My kid knows who Oprah Winfrey is. Jesus.

"He's getting the new console for his birthday. Sounds pretty cool. Of course, his parents, they've got . . . you know . . ." Sonny dropped his voice a little. "Money."

I smiled at that, the way he spoke with such discretion. I'd also caught the way he'd said birthday, though. We couldn't hide the fact it was painful for all of us. You get reminded of how few there might be left.

"Yeah," I said. "Sounds pretty cool." Sonny didn't ask me for a new console, which I think I'd've asked my dad for at his age. I said, "You know, having money's okay, Sonny. It's not a crime. Some people do better than others, that's all. Me and your mum, we do all right. We manage okay."

Sonny set his pad down, the image of a fire fight on the screen frozen for a moment. He looked at me with his big earnest eyes, transfixing me for about the millionth time. There are whole worlds smaller than the possibilities in Sonny's eyes. Fresh after his birth, when I first held him and looked into those amazingly bright pools of blue I knew all my truths had been shown to him, all my lies and indiscretions. There's no room for deceit when you look into Sonny and he looks back at you. Not then, and not now. Heaven floats there sometimes, I'm sure, winking at me and telling me not to be afraid.

But, of course, I am.

His eyes were on me now, a question in them, as he tried to puzzle through something, or at least get it straight.

"Yeah, but we're not rich, are we, Dad?"

"No, we're not rich. But we're better off than a lot of people."

"Dad, you going anywhere tonight?"

"Sure. We're always busy. Got a fare to Manchester Airport from Thirsk. Johnson Cabs to the rescue. Why?"

"I was wondering if you had time for a game or two."

I raised my eyebrows at the frozen creature being zapped on the screen. "On this?"

He nodded and I saw how suddenly pale his face was, how translucent the skin. He had deep shadows under his eyes; he always had, but tonight they were a little browner, a little more for keeps. I heard myself saying, yes, I had time for a couple of games, even as a pounding voice in the back of my head, keeping time with my rapidly beating heart, rammed home its syllables of inevitability.

I pushed all of that away as best I could, the way I

always do.

Let him be all right. Let him have a little longer. Don't let my son die.

I settled in front of the TV screen with the spare joypad and shot some monsters from hell, wishing it were as easy to shoot the real things. What wouldn't I give for Sonny?

A week after I'd picked Chrissie up outside the hotel, I saw the mouse woman on TV. She was shaking up a bottle of champagne, with her husband standing alongside her, and an out-of-work former gameshow host was presenting them with a big cheque the size of a parade banner. They had won three million on the lottery that weekend.

Of course I did a double take seeing that. I thumbed up the volume and listened with loose incredulity to the newsreader saying the woman was Helen Dunn from York and that the first thing she was going to do was take the family on holiday and leave her job as a cleaner at the local hospital. Her husband, a big man with a fleshy face that looked out of place above the suit he probably only wore for weddings and funerals, gurned a grin as his cheeks flushed. He looked as uncomfortable surrounded by media attention as a chimney sweep with the instructions manual to Bill Gates's house.

How about that? The little mouse woman had won her fortune. The odds on that happening must've been longer than me picking Chrissie Rhodes up, right?

It shouldn't bother me. So why did it? And why, when I saw her taking the cheque as she stood in front of a shining Ferrari draped with blonde models in tight white t-shirts and tiny red shorts, did I have a mental flash of Chrissie Rhodes snarling at me through my rear-view mirror?

Perhaps it was the glances of unease that I saw flit between Helen and her husband.

You could probably dismiss them as nervousness in front of the TV crews, but I couldn't help wondering if it was because of something else.

I had an odd feeling that I couldn't shake for the rest of that day. Almost as though I'd seen something that I shouldn't have seen, but which now that I had I should take advantage of. I did the airport run a few times and every now and again I thought about Chrissie telling me she was in sales and I thought about the unhappy mouse woman looking like she'd been caught committing some offence when she realised that I'd seen Chrissie going into her house.

Because it kept bugging me, I couldn't concentrate on my audiobooks when I was driving back from a drop-off. I shut the player down, leaving the radio on in the background, a habit I'd picked up from listening out for the traffic interrupt programme on the stereo. I drove without finding words to give form to my thoughts.

That night I did a search for a Chrissie Rhodes on the internet, using "York" and "England" as key words. I got just under a couple of hundred hits. Great. Maybe there was a way to narrow things down further, though? She had a large folder in her hand, I remembered: artwork of some kind? I put in art and wound up with a sequence of dead ends.

Maybe there was some clue in the business card's logo.

I reached over to the roller holder and flipped through till I found Chrissie's card. It felt as cold as it ever had, a thin slice of cooled magma turned to rock. Only now something was different, there were more words engraved there. Below the *Chrissie Rhodes* was another line of text, smaller than her name, but legible all the same.

Sales.

That was new. There'd not been anything below her name before, I was sure of it.

Okay. Well, this was weird. I held the card up to the light, wondering if there was yet more lettering and the only way to spot it was by angling the card just so. Like one of the holographic superhero posters Sonny used to collect, iridescent lettering might only be visible if the light caught it in just the right way.

I twisted the card around, trying to capture anything there by the glow of the monitor, and then by the USB desk lamp. The card was thin and appeared fragile at first glance, for all that it was sliced rock. But it had a toughness about it, too. Delicate veins sprang to life and glittered as I examined it. Soft brown hues, streaks of golden sandstone, rougher blue areas that looked at once harsh and hostile and then like the feathery clouds of dusk made solid and fallen to earth.

But if there was any other writing I couldn't see it.

Maybe it was me, maybe I'd been tired and either hadn't noticed the second line before or I had done but it had slipped my mind.

I didn't think it likely, but it was always a possibility.

Then why did it bug me, why was I uneasy?

The screensaver took over the monitor, accompanied by the little grunts the computer made as it called up the programme. Sonny used to say it was the computer wizard inside getting a sweat on to make things work. I think he got the idea from installation programmes. Because of that, whenever the computer starts complaining and groaning to itself, I always think of the little guy from *The Wizard of Oz* shifting big levers behind his curtain somewhere inside the PC. Magic's not always what it seems, and it's important to remember that.

The screensaver took my attention away from the card and I moved the mouse to free up the monitor. I typed in Chrissie's name and immediately after it "sales", and then punched the search directive.

Got exactly one hit.

Thursday morning, Sonny was rushed into hospital.

I was driving at the time. Of course I was driving. Sometimes it's all I ever seem to do. I dream of endless journeys without the hope of a destination, just praying for the slim chance that I might be overlooked, that we might be overlooked, and that the world might forget about us and leave us alone for a while. Sonny might live forever then. And so might we.

Bobbi called as I was on the road with a fare, something she would only do if things were serious. I have two mobile phones; one is for general work stuff, always off when I'm driving, and the other I keep switched on all the time. But only Bobbi has the number to it. Its ring is plain and undistinguished, and I dread hearing it with all my being.

I was on my way to the Leeds Bradford airport with a soccer executive in the car when the phone rang. He didn't say anything when I peeled over to the side of the road and answered the call but I could sense his impatience. Right then I didn't much care.

"Yeah? . . . Okay. How bad? . . . Soon as I can."

I hung up and turned to the soccer man, who'd been sitting in silence. He didn't look impressed.

"Look, I'm sorry about this. My son's desperately ill. He's just been taken to Jimmy's and I need to get there as soon as I can. That's why I had to answer the phone."

The set of his face broke. "Okay. If you want you can drop me off wherever you like." He even offered to get out of the car with his luggage and make his own way for the rest of the journey, call another cab if he needed to. I shook my head: the airport was only another couple of minutes away so I insisted on driving him, though I almost flung his shell-case out of the boot at him when we got there. Finishing the fare had given me a chance to get things clear in my head, to calm down a little. The guy wished me the best of luck but I was already jumping back in the car. I turned out of the restricted speed zone and blitzed the roundabouts, drove to Leeds as quickly as I could, fighting off the shakes all the way and telling myself Sonny would be all right, he had to be.

Parking at Jimmy's is never easy. The road leading past the hospital is slow and the car parks invariably filled to bursting. I didn't bother with them, just motored into the main entrance, not altogether surprised when a guy stopped me at the gatehouse to ask where I thought I was going.

"It's my boy, he's just been brought in, he's serious, you know?"

I saw him consider telling me I couldn't park in here, but only for a moment. There must have been something in my expression, because he said, "Okay, pull over on the left and leave me the keys. I'll come find you if you're not out before my shift ends."

I walked through the hospital seeing only a confusion of corridors, making wrong turn after wrong turn as I tried and failed to calm myself enough to take a second to read the signs and at least try and get my bearings. Somewhere in the echoing maze of the building a Jamaican nurse whom I later learned was called Jemima Darling saw the state of me and rather than giving directions took me to where I needed to be. If I'd taken a right rather than a left when I'd come through the main doors I'd've been there in a minute.

"Thank you," I told her. I can't remember if she said anything back to me.

Sonny was hooked up to all sorts of medical apparatus. Tubes and drips snaked into him, coiling around his vitals in support, squeezing breath for him and slinking blood and medicine through his veins, delicately injecting poisons to try and shift what was ailing him. Bobbi was at his bedside, looking ashen and shocked. She took one look at me and was full of apologies.

"I'm sorry, Matt. I was hanging the washing out. I don't know how long he was on the floor. I started talking to Nicola, she and Graham are back from holiday, and the time went I don't know where and I found him and . . ." She couldn't say any more, her mouth just moved around an empty space where words should've been.

"Hey, hey. It's okay. You couldn't have known." I pulled her to me and put my arms around her. She was shaking. Or I was. It was hard to tell which. "It's okay, I promise. It could have happened to either one of us."

We couldn't keep an eye on Sonny twenty-four/seven. It just wasn't possible. Bobbi was upset because it was her watch that it had happened on; I knew it could just as easily have happened when I was with him, and that if it had then I'd feel the way she did now. There was nothing to be sorry about, other than that Sonny was ill in the first place. We both did our best. It was just never enough.

I held her as I looked into her eyes, trying to calm my expression so she knew everything was . . . well, whatever passes for as good as things can be in this kind of situation. I stroked a finger over one of her eyebrows and smoothed her forehead.

"Tell me what they've said."

"In a second. I think I need to . . . I just."

"Take as long as you need."

She cleaned up her face, and I tasted tears where I'd kissed her cheek. I helped her sit down and I took my first proper look at Sonny, never letting go of Bobbi's hand. There was hardly any life to see in his closed eyelids, the slightest twitch that I didn't dare hope meant he was dreaming. He was in deep, sleeping but struggling. His bare chest looked shallow, awfully hollow, too tiny to keep him alive. Little trembles ran the length of him as he fought whatever cheap trick biology had pulled to try and end everything too soon. Pads were taped to him, on his forehead and to his chest, little sucker attachments like the toy arrowheads that went with the Wild West Indian bow I'd played with as a child. Shoot the arrow from one of them and it nearly always missed the target, I remembered. Maybe whatever arrow had been shot his way would miss, too.

The tapes on Sonny's chest were holding in needles, making sure they wouldn't come out; they pierced the flesh, unlike the fallen arrows of my youth, which always fell short of where you were aiming or bounced off your victim without leaving a mark.

Kids' stuff and fantasy conflicts. Bad context.

"Oh Matt. It's not good. He's struggling. They don't know if . . . He's so badly congested. They're trying to clear the whatever it is, the gunk, clear it out."

Bobbi sounded as if fatigue had smothered her. She looked defeated.

"His lungs have filled, so they're pumping him up

with some medicine or other to try and shift it. It's like the stuff . . . It's like the stuff they use with HIV patients. He's full of fluids and when he wakes he's really struggling to breathe. He gulps and it's . . ." She shook her head, managed to compose herself again. "I think he's in pain. It's about getting it all out before it turns too nasty. They're talking about inducing a coma if it gets too bad . . ."

I couldn't speak, not wanting Bobbi to hear my voice fracture, so I nodded that I understood. Sonny wavered before me through my tears. Sunlight dappled my vision and the room swam in and out of sharpness. I leaned over and somehow found myself sitting in one of those moulded visiting chairs you find dotted around hospitals, because my legs wouldn't hold me up any longer, and I started crying. I cried until I found I'd used all my tears up. And then I found you never use them all up; we have so many that they never stop for the ones we love.

Sonny came out of the hospital a week later, waved off by Jemima Darling and a few other nurses. He looked more tired than I'd ever seen him, but he wore his sunshine smile at seeing a new day.

Want the truth? I never thought I'd be coming through the doors with him.

Maybe I'd prayed enough. Maybe God took a moment from His schedule to dispatch an angel to help us out.

But even as I stepped into the parking lot with

Sonny and Bobbi, I couldn't help but think about the next time, and if we'd be so lucky then . . .

That night, I hit the Internet again. I knew it was pointless now (I think perhaps I'd always known that); the doctors at Jimmy's had almost but not quite said as much. The clock had started ticking: we weren't talking years now, we might not even be talking seasons. Months, perhaps. What hope we'd had of Sonny making his teens was all but gone. But what harm was there in looking?

All the usual sites were going through the same old stuff: talking about how there was no money, no serious research right now. I got frustrated and wound up clicking away, scrolling through pages of propaganda and useless contact addresses, hoping for someone new who might help. I found nothing – just pages of ifs and maybes; and ifs and maybes I'd had for most of my child's life.

I read some weblogs, journals by other parents and kids dealing with the same thing Sonny and we were going through. How brave you must be to put so stark a set of experiences where they can be read by anyone. I couldn't do that. I know Bobbi couldn't. But it wouldn't have surprised me to see one by Sonny Johnson on there. There's something about these kids, they have a kind of inner strength that comes from someplace I've never been. Oh sure, they ache, they have their grey days, they even despair at times; but then out of nowhere they find a little something to get them through another 24 hours. Somewhere within themselves they know that with the promise of tomorrow comes the possibility of the infinite, so you might as well enjoy closing your eyes as you go to sleep on the soft, warm pillow the night before . . .

Come three in the morning I was still surfing the web, with tired eyes and a dry mouth barely holding back the yawns; the room was flickering with the shadows of ongoing downloads.

Three in the morning and all your demons come out to haunt you. Anything is possible then.

I tried Chrissie Rhodes's page again, the one link leading to her, and didn't get the Bad Gateway notice this time.

At first it was just the blank screen. The little blue "loading" circle spinning around was the only indication that anything might make a show. Then the screen went black and a familiar image appeared: the same profile of Chrissie Rhodes as the one on her business card, this time white on black. It filled centre screen and that was it. Nothing else. No name, just the stylised profile.

I clicked on it and the image disappeared to be replaced by a menu bar on the left and an animated quill scribbling "Your Name" over and over again on the bottom of a contract written on scrolled parchment.

The parchment – curled into a roll at the top, ending in stylised raggedness at the bottom – filled the rest of the page. The contract was impossible to read clearly, just black squiggles suggesting words above the red "*Your Name*" signature.

I was tired by now and kept glancing at the clock. The knowledge that I had a client to take up to Newcastle by midday clawed at the back of my head.

Not much longer, I thought. Just a while to check out the menu options and then I'll get to bed. I knew I wouldn't disturb Bobbi by going up this late. Long years of driving at night had taught us how to accommodate the other's sudden presence after a few hours' absence. Bobbi could sleep through me getting under the covers with her in that strange hinterland of time when it's neither late at night nor early in the morning but someplace between the two. She'd be aware, somewhere at the periphery of wakefulness, that I'd joined her at last, and sometimes she might turn over to put her arm around me, or else snuggle her back up closer, pushing herself against my chest and lap as we eased together to share some warmth.

I read the options on the menu bar, thinking I'd go up to join her in a while.

"About." "Offers." "What's New." "Contact."

I clicked on "About" and read a small and not very illuminating biography of Chrissie that pretty much said she was Chrissie Rhodes and she was the Northern England representative and sales person of the Company (that's how they referred to themselves throughout the text, the Company, capital "C", nothing more specific) and had been in the job for the last six months. There was no way of telling how recently the page had been updated, so I took that six months loosely. Chrissie could've been working in York for the last year or more for all I knew.

Moving back to the menu bar, I pressed the "Offers" option. This time there was more text to read, but it was all baffling. It spoke about clauses and sub-clauses, minor perditionary discounts and so on. It was as far as I could make out nonsensical and baseless, like something from a Kafka novel. Officialese out of context, Catch-22 with all the footnotes.

The "What's New" page was making a big thing about their direct point of sale. The Company now offered a direct to the door sales representative and complete in-home contract negotiations at your place of domicile or at any other location convenient to you. Full discretion guaranteed. Which was maybe why Helen Dunn had been less than pleased to see me parked outside her home.

Try as I could to find out, the webpage neglected to mention what the Company was actually selling.

I stretched and extended a silent yawn toward the ceiling. This was hopeless and a waste. I was thinking dumb thoughts.

It was late or it was early; whichever, I needed to get some sleep. Finally, out of stubborn doggedness as much as anything else, I clicked the "Contact" icon and watched a new mail message open on the monitor, with the email address already inserted, "chrissie_rhodes.612@h.o.t.company.mail.com".

Well, there was no way I was emailing her, especially not at this hour. I didn't even know what I wanted to say to her.

"Hi. Remember me? I was the private hire cab that stopped for you when I shouldn't have done, in the rain, a while back. How you doing? By the way, did you help Helen Dunn win three million on the lottery? And if so, what other services do you offer?"

I ought to shut the PC down and go to bed. Tired eyes and slow thought processes – they swoop in and get you when it's past three in the morning, are never a good combination. Really, I should just shut the machine down; there wasn't any need to put Chrissie's name in my address book before I did that . . . Why would I want to? What could she possibly offer that I'd have any use for now?

When I woke the next morning I had mail. The usual spam, a couple of enquiries, and three bookings. And there was something else in my private account.

Something from Chrissie Rhodes with the subject heading "The Sonny Package".

I should have written her off as a crank and deleted her message. That's what I was thinking as I sat in the hotel restaurant, waiting to meet her a couple of days later. But whenever I tried to think like that an image of the mousy woman came back to me, Helen Dunn staring at me as though she'd been caught putting flies in the schoolteacher's lunchbox. Closely followed by an image of her looking uncomfortable beneath the smile she wore as she accepted the lottery cheque.

But the truth is this: if you're in a desperate enough place, all possible avenues of escape have to be explored.

I'd parked near Clifford's Tower and walked the rest of the way to the hotel. It wasn't far, and the stroll through the tourists gave me a chance to clear my head and think about what Chrissie had written in her email, to try and grasp the implications if she were serious – if it was even *possible* for her to be serious – and not some nut getting her kicks out of other people's pain.

Again, though, whenever I thought like that, everything came down to one thing: Helen Dunn and the champagne and Ferrari, her cheque for three million pounds.

Chrissie had left instructions on how to get in touch with her in her email, to discuss further arrangements, and here I was. But if you're thinking that I'd done all of this without talking to Bobbi about it, then you're wrong. I printed out Chrissie's email and showed it to her before I took my first ride of the day. I didn't say anything as she read. Told her we'd talk about it when I got back that evening and not to dismiss it out of hand because . . . Well, because I'd seen the mouse woman's expression when she saw me watching her. But I couldn't tell Bobbi that.

Not just then.

Chrissie had somehow known I'd looked through her site and had mailed me with an initial proposal on behalf of the Company. The contract would be binding if signed, but up till then all negotiation stances were open to Bobbi and me. We just had to decide what the best deal we could get was. The rest would be left to Chrissie's people. There was a guarantee that any contract would be null and void if they couldn't complete what they'd undertaken to do before any mitigating circumstances intervened.

They meant that if Sonny died then we were off the hook and wouldn't have to pay. So whatever they wanted, the house, the insurance, the cab company, the whole of my income for the rest of my working life, it wouldn't be taken from me, from us, in such circumstances.

When I got home that evening after I'd done all my taxiing Bobbi was waiting for me. She didn't say anything as I played with Sonny, who was on a bit of a downer as far as his energy levels were concerned, and waited until he'd gone up to bed and we'd said goodnight to him. The unspoken email was always there, though, as we did a bunch of evening things, raked up the leaves in the garden, washed the dishes, sat through a TV soap and watched a wildlife documentary and then a couple of situation comedies that didn't raise a laugh from either of us. As I pulled Sonny's bedroom door to – we always kept it open a sliver so he could call for us if he needed to, or in case we just wanted to stand and listen to him breathe at night – Bobbi put a finger up to my lips to stop me saying anything too soon and led me downstairs.

She'd turned the TV off and the living room was curtained and softly lighted in pastel shades by the muted glow of the wall sconces. We would be talking in pale hues of indigo, the invisible colour. Already the house seemed a little quieter with Sonny in bed. Here and there, his toys were scattered about the room, and I got the sudden shock of loss I usually get when I'm the only one awake in the house and I think about what it will be like when there's no one left to play with them. What will we do then, pack them up and parcel them off to a charity store, or leave them boxed and gathering dust in the attic, never to be touched again? It's always the same: when Sonny leaves the room it expands to announce its emptiness.

"Come on, Matt. Here, sit down."

Bobbi had rested the hard copy of Chrissie's email on the coffee table. I sat on the comfy cushion beside her on the sofa, not saying anything, just thinking about how this looked, what I'd printed out to show her . . . and how silly it had seemed throughout the day, how stupid I felt for even thinking it was possible. There'd been moments when I'd thought of calling Bobbi and telling her not to read the mail again, just throw the print-up in the bin, I was being stupid, wasn't thinking straight.

But again, with the lights down low and the prospect of another long night filled with anxiety dreams and the fear of waking to what would be the first of the worst days of my life, it didn't seem so stupid any more.

"Bobbi, I know this all seems a bit—" I was going to say silly, ridiculous, any number of adjectives that dismissed the email in front of us. But I didn't get the chance. Bobbi spoke before I could get that far.

"Is there any chance this is for real?"

"I . . ."

"Matt. Please. Tell me. Is there a chance this is for real?"

Sonny gets his eyes from his mother. Bobbi's are big and blue and shiny most of the time, but of late they'd been tired and dull. The strain of Sonny's illness getting worse had taken the gleam away from Bobbi. Now it was back, charged with – I don't know . . . a kind of desperation that anything this absurd might just be possible. Her eyes were imploring me to say I thought that yes, there could be a cure for Sonny here somehow, that miracles wore the faces of pretty women standing out in the rain waiting for a passing cab.

"I don't know how she got in contact. I" – I shook my head, trying to remember the previous night a little better; so much of it was blurred by the overwhelming tiredness of so many late nights. Had I sent an email? I was pretty sure I'd only stored the address, and even then I hadn't written anything in any message box – "I didn't mail her or anything, she got in touch with me. And I didn't give her any details about Sonny, that's for sure. She could have seen the appeal sticker when she was in the cab. I pointed out my picture on the license, probably because I was a little nervous at picking someone up. And it's right beside that. She might have noticed it then. But it seems a bit of a vindictive thing to do, hunting the email address down and offering us a cure."

"She could've taken one of your cards from the

back of the cab."

"I thought of that. But she emailed me on my private address, not the company one, and that's not on the card. She might've found it on a website somewhere, but she would've had to have known what Sonny was suffering from to be so specific in her mail. It's a lot of research for a practical joke."

Bobbi held her hands up and spread her fingers in a baffled gesture.

"Then why us, Matt? Why's she got in touch with us like this?"

Feeling helpless, I said the only thing I could, the only honest answer I had. "I don't know."

"But you must believe there's something to what she says if you've shown me the damn thing."

"The woman Chrissie visited, I saw the look in her eye when she saw me parked up opposite her house. She was scared, embarrassed. She looked caught out, Bobbi. Whatever Chrissie Rhodes was doing there it wasn't a hundred per cent on the straight. I think . . . I think she must work for people who have either really good connections and can make things happen, or . . . Oh, I don't know. Or else she's in league with some kind of gangster operation or something as stupid and ridiculous as that. I just don't *know*, that's what I'm saying. Whichever way you look at it, though, the Dunns are three million better off for it, away on their round the world cruise or whatever it is they're doing. And now this Chrissie woman's knocking on our door with a . . ."

. . . chance of a lifetime?

. . . a cure?

Silence and eye contact, a drowsing house holding its breath, before Bobbi said anything.

"You're making assumptions. You can't be sure the Dunn woman didn't win that money legitimately."

But I was. I was sure. That's why I'd driven into town today. It was why I was here now, sitting at a table waiting for my meeting with Chrissie. To see what she had to offer.

A minute after we were due to meet and I was getting nervous (or perhaps, now that I look back on it, feeling a little thankful and darkly exhilarated) that she wouldn't show up, Chrissie arrived.

Bobbi had Sonny with her all day; they were going to go see a movie, a superhero flick, and I'd agreed I'd phone her when the show was over. I'd let her know how it had gone at the meeting and tell her just what Chrissie wanted. But how do you tell someone about something like this?

I was outside the hotel, walking back to the car, hardly conscious of the many people on the street. Late afternoon segueing into evening, the sky lowering, bladed with darkness. I wonder now that I was even capable of finding my way back to my car and didn't get totalled by a bus or fall through an open manhole cover.

I nearly walked into a guy selling roasted chestnuts

out of a mobile stall and he frowned at me and asked me if I'd like something warm all over my shirt. I whirled away from him, palming an apology distractedly, and carried on moving. I crossed King's Square and went down the Shambles realising that I was at least heading in the right general direction and made a turn to get back to the parking area. The traffic was heavy as usual, a barely moving stream of metal and headlights, taillights and exhaust fumes; but hurrying along the pavements didn't feel like it usually did, as though you were sucking up industrial waste and gumming your lungs together. Everything felt odd and disconnected, the early moon was a leering, canted face above the stepped, uneven roofs that drooped and sloped over the streets; demons flew through the air and whipped at coattails, swung around dusty chimney pots – or was that just the wind and my overburdened imagination?

Clifford's Tower was already lit. It looks made out of butter in the dark, blooming out of the top of its mound like a mushroom. Soft lights and old fortifications, full of the ghosts of a group of people who were set alight years ago. All part of York's unhealthy history. Whatever danced in the shadows out of my view could stay there. I headed over to the car, not stumbling, but definitely sweating. I realised I hadn't needed to rush now it was past six and the parking charges were no longer in force. I could spare myself the time to calm down.

What was I supposed to say to Bobbi? I couldn't tell her the truth. I just couldn't. It was too much. It was insane to even think about it.

Chrissie had walked into the restaurant wearing a different outfit from the one she had on in the cab; this time she was in a Chanel power suit, but she still looked every inch as good as the last time I'd seen her. She carried a slim briefcase and when she extended her large-fingered hand I shook it without thinking. It was as velvety as I'd imagined it would be when I first saw her. Her fingers wrapped over the back of my hand, a *long* way around the back of my hand. Creepy, given the context, the things I hadn't allowed myself to articulate, not even in my most secret thoughts. She had a grip like an industrial compressor.

"Hello, Matt."

"Chrissie."

Someone had already taken her coat. I still had my jacket with me, draped over the back of the seat. This place was expensive and I felt out of my depth, but Chrissie looked right at home. There was a gleam in her eyes as she noticed how uncomfortable I was here. A waiter glided over as soon as she'd taken her seat and looked as though she'd gotten comfortable. Smooth and condescending when he'd seen me alone earlier, he embodied swish charm and servility itself now. He produced menus and left us to think about what we might like to order as he arranged drinks.

Chrissie didn't say a word to me, just leafed through the listings. I felt a tick in my jaw as I tried to get things started. "Okay," I said. "I'm here and—"

"We should order first, Matt. It's more civilised."

I wasn't here to be made fun of, we were talking

about my son, and if there was any malign intent behind Chrissie hauling me over here, then so help me . . .

"Chrissie, I want to know—"

I felt a presence hovering at my shoulder. The waiter was back so I shut up. Chrissie had already decided what she wanted and ordered confidently and without hesitation. I fumbled the menu to the first page and picked something that looked familiar and hopefully not too expensive. I didn't know who was paying for this, but I figured it was probably going to be me.

The waiter sashayed away, leaving us alone again.

"Look Chrissie, I don't know what you want or what you think you're playing at, but I'm in no position to pay you millions. If you're some sort of deranged fantasist or if this's about what happened in the cab—"

She shook her head. "It's a simple enough transaction. Everything that's needed to cure Sonny can be yours. And for that we only want your soul, Matt. Or Bobbi's. I know, I know – we could be greedy, we could take both of you. After all, we're talking about saving your son here, and I think you'd both give all you had for him. But we do like to play fair. Despite what you've heard. Our public relations aren't what they ought to be. But we're working on it."

"What?"

For a moment I thought I'd misheard her, but when she confirmed what she'd just said I knew I was wasting my time. Out in the open, spoken of so casually, it didn't carry the weight of truth, whatever the suspicions I might have harboured that this was what it might come down to.

"No," I said. "No."

"It makes sense if you think about it," she said. "All you've learned about me, the things that didn't seem to fit. Give it a moment and it'll come to you. That realisation. All I'm doing here is skipping the preliminaries. Saving us both some time. I could play it out, but frankly I'm not sure I want to. What did you expect – an angel? At heart you know what I'm representing."

"You're crazy," I told her. "This's been a complete waste." A waste of hope, and the straining, coiled hunger for the impossible. "You're trying to tell me I'm sitting in a hotel restaurant with a woman who thinks she's Satan's emissary, his sales rep. Well, I'll tell you, Chrissie, if the Devil has all the good tunes, he sure needs to work on his sales technique."

I smiled at her, but it was a spoiled smile, one twisted with a dashed, luckless cruelty. I could feel tears prickling my vision but I wouldn't allow them. I placed the desserts menu I found I was holding flat on the tabletop and leaned back in my chair, feeling a little more comfortable, if deflated, now that I knew I wouldn't be here too long.

She was a loony tunes or one of those strange human beings who enjoyed tormenting people. Maybe there's no difference. I could stand up and leave any time I wanted and not be any the worse off for it. Save perhaps the price of the meal.

Chrissie reached down into her folder and produced a sheaf of papers. They were glossy, brochure quality prints, the kind of thing you'd expect to see in a furniture showroom. Only these had weird symbols on them, bastardisations of the zodiac, Olde English scripts written inside out, Ogham lettering. It was the sort of stuff I'd seen on the webpage.

"You could go now, Mathew. But you'll never know if what I'm saying is true or not. There'll be long dark nights ahead of you if you leave. You'll always have that niggling worry and doubt. What if she was telling me the truth."

"I don't know if anyone's ever told you, but you don't look like a demon. Don't have the horns, don't have razorblade teeth or the pitchfork with you – unless you checked it with your coat when you got here." I figured a pointy tail was out of the question, and despite her good looks, I wasn't interested in hunting down a third nipple . . . She looked exactly as I'd seen her when she'd been waiting under the hotel awning. Only her clothes were different and her hair was dry this time. Her scent was the same, warm and spicy – the only hint she came from an infinitely hotter place than this, assuming she did.

She was still playing it straight. "We get dressed up for business."

"Of course you do. So how's it going, you working for the Devil?"

"Here's what we're offering. Of course, we're open to negotiations. The precise details. Just what we can do for each other."

I didn't pick up what she pushed my way; I was too busy looking in her eyes. She wasn't joking. Or if she was then she was doing it very well, with complete sincerity. I couldn't figure her. What did she want? There was no way I was going to go for this; she must know that. Demons and pacts with the Devil, blues guitarists at the crossroads? No one believes in that stuff any more. You're as likely to see elves and pixies complaining about the entrance fee to York Minster as you are to glimpse visitations from the chief fiend on the streets of a city older than Christ.

And yet I was here because I'd been clinging to the hope of the impossible . . .

"Read it, Matt."

When it was obvious she wasn't going to break her gaze and look away from me, I glanced at what she'd placed before me. Documents and slide charts, flow diagrams and texts with all manner of sub-clauses similar to the ones I'd read on the webpage, only this time it was more blatantly bound up in the paraphernalia of witchcraft and demonology.

"So what? Go on, tell me. What's it supposed to mean, Chrissie? I'm supposed to sit here and look at this and come away convinced you can cure my son?" I shrugged. "Sorry. I don't believe a word of it."

"You will, Matt. I'm very good at my job."

"Convince me, then, why don't you."

I thought it was going to end there. This was where the charade had to come to a close. But it didn't. Her expression, up until now almost entirely neutral, as if our last parting hadn't been on any ill terms at all, flared, and she showed a hint of the maliciousness I'd seen in her before.

She said, "All right. You did ask for it."

"Oh, this should be — "

She clicked her fingers and the room froze. At first I didn't realise anything had changed, but even the surge of air that was pushed before people walking around the room turned to icy immobility. The noise of other diners shrank and was gone. I spun my head around, left to right, right to left. Whoa. Strange. What was this?

"Here we go," Chrissie said. "Do enjoy."

Movement returned to the room. The lights dimmed and guttered, the big open fireplace flared from within and cast the only fresh light about us. A face appeared in the new flames, indistinct and ambiguous, but then sickeningly apparent. It was a face made from a thousand flies being burned at once – you could hear their wings frazzling – a hundred claws and wings, horns and barbed tongues, coils and reptile eyes swarming and flaring. I wanted to turn away, but the apparition was too compelling to look away from.

Then it was gone, and I felt myself lurch out of whatever mesmerism had held me to that distorted visage.

Chrissie leaned closer to me and spoke. Two words.

"It's true."

And it was. And it got worse. Milton's most fevered pandemonium erupted around us. What had remained frozen after Chrissie clicked her fingers and the fire danced – the other diners, the waiters, life as it had been before – turned to motion again. But there was more.

Demons danced in the restaurant. I don't know where they came from, but they cavorted amongst the ignorant diners, who somehow went about their business without realising monsters filled these walls. *Demons*. Actual god-awful demons.

One plucked a steak from a dish and slid it between spread buttocks puckering with a pulsing anus, before placing it back where it had lifted it from; others pulled long flaccid pricks on the floor, squirting jism as they trailed behind them like the forked tails of legend.

They were uncouth and horrible, starving beings that I intuitively understood were quick to nourish themselves from the petty slights we administer to each other every day now that they were being given reign in this world by Chrissie. They leaped and capered in a frenzied dance of joy.

A demon with thin spent breasts like the flaps of an envelope leaned across a table and pushed them to the face of an old lady, forcing the nipples into her partly open mouth, and then rocked the woman's head back and forth. As she pulled away, I saw rheumy milk trickle from the old lady's lips. A being who most resembled a shorn monkey took piles of its prodigious dung from the floor, where it ridged ever higher in a steaming pyramid, and dispersed it at random over the plates of the restaurant's patrons.

These beasts were not quiet as they went about their work, oh no . . . God, the sounds . . . They chattered, moving their maws as they stretched sinew to the point it must snap, they sawed their hind-legs together like crickets, they screamed and cried, produced sounds that were nothing more pleasant than a stiletto blade inserted into the eardrum over and over again.

I pressed my hands to my head to hide the worst from my ears but nothing could stop them. I squeezed my eyes closed, dipped my head, groaned long and loudly . . .

How long it all went on, I don't know. It felt like hours. It felt like *years*. Finally, when I was certain I could bear no more and that I was in hell already, the pantomime of depravity stopped.

I'm not sure if Chrissie clicked her fingers again, but the room was back to how it had been only moments before; no one seemed to have noticed the interruption and the uninvited guests. I took my hands from my ears, opened my eyes, looked around, frantic for a second. No one had seen the demons, they had left as quickly as they had come. But there were signs of their having been here. The dung monkey's shit was still on plates, being spooned and forked into mouths by diners who couldn't see or apparently taste it, though they chewed a little more on the food before swallowing it. The old lady who'd had the demon's breasts in her mouth was wiping a serviette across her lips as if to remove a taste for which she couldn't quite account. But apart from those hints no one seemed aware in the slightest that anything unusual had gone on. The lights were as bright as ever, the fire coughed and then continued to burn normally. Satan and his minions had left the building, except for . . .

"It's true, Mathew."

I looked at her, I looked at the Devil's sales representative as she forked a heap of dung from her plate and inserted it between her glamorous lips and started chewing. Her eyes danced, alive with a smile, mocking me as she waited for me to do what I would do next.

A week after my meeting with Chrissie, Sonny was taken into hospital again. This time he went into the coma they'd feared he'd succumb to the last time he was there. The one they were scared would set in if the fluids in his lungs couldn't be drained. It wasn't an artificial coma, of the type they'd thought about inducing last time. It was the real thing.

It looked like we were nearing the end.

Did I regret not taking up Chrissie's offer of a cure? It would only have cost me my soul, something I never really believed existed before I'd met her.

But that was the thing; that was where she'd failed: she made me believe.

Without Chrissie's parade of demons I'd not have thought twice about signing a document entitling someone to my soul if he or she could cure Sonny. As far as I was concerned they'd be getting at best a notion, a theosophical possibility, whereas I'd be getting a long shot, a final no-hope chance of a cure for my child. A gesture that made me feel good. Perhaps some crazy placebo that could be communicated to Sonny from my belief in a dumb document that I'd signed. Ridiculous, but sometimes you never know what you might get.

The truth was that Chrissie had overplayed her hand. Her vindictiveness got the better of her. Showing me things she knew would threaten my sanity, all because I'd caught her hunting through her handbag in my cab. Because I had, for a single unconsidered moment, spied on her. That's why she brought on that pageant of depravity in the hotel. And that's where she lost me.

I was tempted for a moment, realising what was on offer, I'll be honest. Tempted to sign away my soul for Sonny. But the shock and fear of what she'd shown me told me there were worse things in the world than losing my boy.

If demons existed, then so too must souls, and souls could – *must* – be eternal. Why else would the Devil be so hungry for them? So why not take the pain of losing Sonny, knowing full well that there'd be more after his flesh fouled and decomposed, and not just an end? If there's a place of eternal damnation then surely there's its opposite, too. I could live with that, and I could even let Sonny die with that, however hard it would be.

Exchange eternity for a few earthly years? There were some things I just couldn't give up.

But, God, it wasn't easy. Seeing my boy in pain and then in the final moments of stillness, approaching the moment of extinction. That's hard.

Bobbi was a shell. Nothing lived inside her for a while, and I feared I might lose her, too.

Tell me, how can we have the ones we love torn

away from us and not go insane? Before the encounter with Chrissie, I'd've said there was nothing for us once Sonny had gone. We'd wind up as medicated corpses walking the world, numb to truth and feeling. But now . . . Now I think I know how to avoid going crazy. For want of a better word I can only call it faith, the old standby of the Sunday school merchants and pulpit preachers; something people raise as a comfort against all ends. But without whatever faith is, and I still couldn't *define* it for you, that thing that was keeping me going then, despite all I've seen and what I suspect and believe that I *know* about souls, then what more do we have? How can someone without that survive the losses?

Bobbi wasn't religious in any way, she didn't have faith. And however much you reason with someone and explain to them that it's all right, that there's something more than this existence of flesh and despair, you can never prove it. Not without demonstrations from the Devil's representative on earth. Even though I sometimes glimpsed apparitions in the hospital corridors, hideous cloaked entities floating through the deserted streets in the darkest hours of a barbed night, what possible good could it do to tell her when I could prove none of it? I just hoped my faith in more than this physical existence would somehow communicate itself to her and help her.

That's what I had to do for her, let her find her own way and support her.

Bobbi barely functioned after I'd told her about Chrissie and what I said happened at our meeting. I told her Chrissie was a sham, that the entire thing was a bad joke, a new insurance policy scam.

What else could I have said? The truth? She'd think I was crazy with grief.

I didn't mention the demons, and I couldn't begin to explain what had gone on in that hotel restaurant. I wouldn't have been able to frame the words even if I wanted to.

All the same, I think Bobbi knew there was more to it than spiel and con tricks. There are things that are impossible to hide from someone whose life you've shared the number of years we have shared ours.

With Sonny in the hospital, we spent the majority of our time there, letting my parents take turns at visiting him, and then going up together, Bobbi and me, and at times individually nearer the end, trying as much as was possible to have one of us present, so that if it looked like Sonny was going to go then we could call the other up and both be there.

My father would sit in for spells by himself, helping out if we couldn't manage the hours, and telling the sleeping Sonny stories we doubted he'd be able to hear. Bobbi's parents had emigrated years ago, but they kept in touch by phone to see how things were going, even suggested flying halfway around the world to be with us. This time we didn't turn them down; we knew if they weren't here for when Sonny died then they'd at least be here for the funeral. Even if all else was gone, they wouldn't want to miss that.

* * *

Hospital hours. A null time of nothingness.

Things dragged on longer than I could have expected, and yet it didn't seem to be long enough. The inevitable was coming. But in its own hour. Of its own volition. We were just there, eating up the pain, feeling every second.

I'd cry without realising I was doing so; suddenly putting my hands to my face to find them coming away wet with tears, or my lips unexpectedly stung by saltwater. I assumed Bobbi cried as well, when she was alone. But she made her eyes as hard as iron when anyone else was around. She held a quiet determination in her bones, but I still felt a sense of shock and emptiness about her.

Then the emptiness changed, became something else, and I had questions to which I didn't want to hear the answers.

One night last week, I'd driven home, wondering again how long it would be till this was over. Sonny had made it through another night, another day. How long could he go on fighting like that? I didn't know. I pulled to a stop in the middle of the road outside the house, wondering at the big car half blocking the entrance to the driveway. There's a certain kind of arrogance in people who do that, an inconsideration; it's like the guys who park in the disabled zone because they can't be bothered to walk an extra twenty feet. It's the same sort of thing as the Mercs and Beamers not letting you into traffic. Only the big guys do it, skew their twelve valve in front of your driveway so you can't get in or out. But I couldn't find any anger. By now, with everything that was going on in my life, I'd run out of feelings.

Because I couldn't be bothered with it all, I just pulled the car half up onto the pavement a little down the road; I didn't want to go knocking on doors to find the guy and get him to shift his car.

I'd just cranked the handbrake and shut off the engine, exhaled a sigh so pitiful I felt it might drip with rain, when I glanced in the nearside wing mirror and saw her come out of the house.

Familiar suit, familiar hair, familiar folder in her hand.

My heart stilled. Bobbi quietly closed the door behind her and Chrissie walked down my drive and got in the passenger side of the waiting car. She hadn't seen me; or if she had then she didn't acknowledged me. The car started up, its rear lights glowing red in the evening dark as it passed me. The windows were steamed black. I hadn't realised there was a driver waiting behind the wheel when I'd driven by. I watched it pull away. The red lights weren't grinning when the car reached the end of the street and took a left turn; there was just a push on the brake pedal, a slowing before the corner that made them glow momentarily brighter; they weren't winking at me at all.

I couldn't move. I was stuck fast where I was.

It began to rain, coming down hard and suddenly, and I thought about my first impressions of Chrissie Rhodes, that she was the kind of girl who could make the heavens sing. How wrong could you be? Wail maybe, cry in sorrow, but never sing.

I waited a while, lit a cigarette, something I haven't done since we first started taking Sonny for the tests, and sat smoking with the window down. After I'd finished I flicked the butt outside, where it fell to the wet road, hissing out its life. I started the car and drove around the estate a few times, and then up the drive, going into the garage and closing the door behind me. I didn't say anything to Bobbi, just smiled and hugged her, my heart beating so hard I thought she must feel it against my ribs and know I knew. If she didn't notice that, surely she'd see how badly I was shaking. But I'd been shaking about a lot of things of late.

"He's all right?"

I nodded. "Yeah. Made it through okay. My dad's with him now, another story through the night."

She smiled at that, a little sadly, and I wondered what she'd done.

But I couldn't ask. I was scared she might tell me.

I wandered into the garage/office and searched my roller holder, failing at first to find the card I was hunting for. When I looked a second time it was there, but in the wrong section. I'd left it in the business addresses index intending to throw it away after my meeting with Chrissie but never got around to it. Now it was in the family/friends file.

I wanted to believe I had put it there by accident. I wanted to believe that oh so much. *God, how I wanted it to be true.* I couldn't face the thought that Bobbi had taken it without telling me and mistakenly put it back there. I could persuade my heart to stop thumping so harshly if I believed that I was the person who'd put that card in that file. I took it out and held it, not knowing what to do, before thinking I'd return it to the business index when I was done. But then I thought, *Why take the risk?* Why not throw it away right now?

I looked at it a while before coming to a decision. There was more writing there, below the *Chrissie Rhodes* and the *Sales.* There was now a phone number. At first there had been only the name, then the sales, and now . . .

As I held the card up to the light I watched the individual digits of the number begin to fade from sight. I squinted to try to get the last few, but I missed them. Goddamn it! Suddenly I wanted that phone number. Jesus, but there might still be time . . .

If anything had been signed, if any contract had been inked, we could still cancel, right?

Except now the *Sales* was fading, too, and then Chrissie's name as well. Until the card became less and less substantial and its constituent pieces came apart, crumbling and then fragmenting to powder.

In under a second there was nothing left, not even grains of sand.

I knew I was wasting my time, but I tried anyway. I fired up the PC, went online, clicked through my stored history, and found the address I wanted. Saw the Bad Gateway message on the webpage, found the hurried email that I scribbled out in a mad fury of loose key-strokes to Chrissie Rhodes bounce right back to me.

That had been last week. Now . . . well, now things have changed.

Sonny has made a quick recovery, surprising nearly everyone. But his mother didn't seem that surprised, more grateful really than anything else, sort of satisfied. Some of the doctors say these things happen, though they can't say why: recoveries out of nowhere. It just happens now and again, to all kinds of people in all kinds of places. No reason why, just be thankful. Call it a miracle if you like.

That's what they say.

Call it a miracle.

It happens sometimes, huh?

I find myself wondering how many times. I find myself speculating about the number of visits that the loved ones of those ill children and sick husbands and desperately ill wives have had from someone representing the Company. Men and women being offered a way out of what they thought was the worst thing that could possibly happen to them, when medical science had failed them. Miracle cures. And all it will cost is . . .

What was Chrissie Rhodes doing coming out of my house with a sly, satisfied smile on her face? Had she got what she'd been looking for from the first, when she'd slid into the back of my cab, steaming as the rain had burned off her? Was it Bobbi she'd wanted, right from the very beginning of all of this?

Don't even think about it.

But it's hard not to. It really is.

And so each day I watch Sonny, just as I always have. I watch to see if he continues to grow healthier. I watch for signs he might suffer a relapse. I look into Bobbi's eyes and see that they're shining again, but with a patina of iron scattered across them that doesn't invite questions. And despite everything I find that I'm hopeful and hoping. Hopeful and hoping.

Even if I couldn't tell you what it is that I'm hoping for.

tied up good
and true

Where to begin on Mulberry's cruelties?

The list of his misdemeanours was a long one, and the reading of it fit only for those whose eyes had been hardened to the terrible deeds one human being could inflict upon another. Even then I would be loath to suggest that such a soul could come away untroubled from its study.

Some records are appalling and best consigned to lead-lined vaults, left there never to be opened; and yet, come the time it was full, Mulberry's file would need burying beneath a volcano. It was already stuffed to the gills with the most devious of tortures, some small, some large, from his early years and on into adulthood. For pages and pages that list extended in a lexicon of injustices, itemising paltry cruelties and twists of relished vindictiveness, underscoring hurts and slanders administered with volatile delight. And that was only the beginning. Come its incomplete end (and it should be said that the list was only incomplete because there was potentially so much more to come, Mulberry being not yet out of his middle years and his imagination not truly unleashed), butchers would put away their cleavers and take up brushes to paint bucolic watercolour scenes, warmongers would plant flowers in the muzzles of their weapons and throw away their uniforms of conflict for ever.

The truth was clear: to the mortal eye there was not a smidgen of loveliness about Mulberry's crimes, however original they might be and no matter how much they were performed with the beginnings of a creative flourish. He was an adept little monster, a practitioner of stealing dreams and putting in their place nothing but nightmares. And he did it in the worst ways he could conceive.

I first met him when I was wearing the form of an unsure young man, lacking direction or the confidence to strike forth a route of his own, away from those old familiar ties and the expectations of his upbringing. Each morning before I'd traipse into Quinlan's Bar to begin work the mirror showed me an openly naïve and youthful face behind round, Jon-Boy Walton eyeglasses, whisker-less cheeks quick to flower with roses of embarrassment, hair the colour of straw, strong teeth not quite snaggled, and a gait that twitched with the awkwardness of the perpetually clumsy.

Here was someone uncomfortable in his skin, lost in his clothing like a child in an adult's outfit, one who had been sent into the world to do a man's job without the first instruction of how to go about it.

A victim, just waiting to be ensnared by a person

like Mulberry True.

Perhaps Mulberry's sort can scent prey on the wind, track it through even the foulest weather and come to land on it; or else there is some psychic element that communicates to the wolf the presence of a nearby lamb – because into the bar he walked, while I was alone and looking forlorn and lost, about my work of shining glasses and washing the counter top with a limp cloth rag.

I glanced up to see him enter and returned to my polishing, a bashful shyness upon me as I recognised the beast hiding within the lines of his anatomy. It was, in its own seemingly insignificant way, as if I had been waiting for him to find me.

Business was slow so early in the day, though it would pick up come the lunch hour, and the bar was regularly crowded after three. With snow falling on the streets like the shredded epidermis of clouds and the carollers not yet out, early December was but a hum on the song of the year. The sole pair of customers who'd visited the bar that morning had left a good half hour earlier. But I knew there'd be more of them later; an open door and the prospect of a drink to warm the insides never left even the most dismal hostelry empty for long.

Feigning attention to my task, I watched Mulberry pass the empty tables and noted the way his eyes recorded the lack of business in the bar. He wore an expression calculatedly free of guile as he approached me.

His was an open face at a glance, wide and passing

cheerful, somewhere in the landmine-strewn fields of his middle forties. Not a clue revealed what that face had grinned at, how it had laughed at acts depraved and disgusting. It was a face that did not allow for a show of the monstrous, but it could be seen there all the same, if you knew how to look for it.

He crossed the room to the counter.

"Hey," he said to me and spread his weight on a stool. He took off his bulky jacket and laid it over the vacant perch beside him. "Cold day. Enough to freeze them off. I'm Mulberry True. How you doing?"

"Jackson Good," I told him, nodding. "I'm okay, sir."

"Pleased to meet you, Jackson Good." He patted a big hand on the bar top, heaved a satisfied sigh, and then he looked around. "Pretty quiet today, huh?"

"It picks up later." I managed to say this with little evidence of the Good family's habitual stutter. "Get you something?"

"You sure can. What've we got?"

I listed the drinks, bottled on the shelves and strung up in optics and on tap in front of him. I heard the nerves in my voice, in case I forgot something. I wasn't so long in the job that I knew all the details, the things I needed to remember. So much was new to me.

"No, no. That's no good," he said, interrupting my flat and somewhat stumbling rendition of the malt whiskeys we stocked. "Jackson, I've endured enough."

"Sir?"

"What you should be doing, Jackson, it's not reading off a list you memorised. You should be enthusing, making it sound like something that a man would *want* to drink. Something he'd *salivate* about."

"Uh, salivate, Mister True?"

"Mulberry," he corrected. "And yes goddamn it, salivate. You know the word? Uh huh. Make a man think you've something he'd like to have. So that if he can't pay for it he'll want to take it anyway. And if he can't take it away from you, he'll want to do something for you – you just have to name it – *anything* so he can get his hands on what you've tempted him with. Psychology, son. It's all a part of selling."

"Well, I don't know about that. I'm just a barkeep, Mister True. And not a very good one, I'll be honest. This is only my second week in the job."

"No one's *just* anything, Jackson. Remember that."

"Yes, sir, I'll try." I stood by helplessly, unsure as to what to do next, wondering if I should carry on reciting the remaining whiskeys or wait for him to select a drink.

Hunching over to bring me into the aura of his confidence, as if he were extending an invitation to include me in a conspiracy, he said, "Let's try again, see if we can do this properly." He held my gaze, and when I didn't say anything he sank back onto his stool, smiling openly. "Come on – read me the list, and *sell* it this time, for goodness' sake. Really sell it."

We did – or I did – and he made a choice, though I could see that he was still unconvinced by my sales technique. I poured him a beer, put a couple of shots beside it, like he'd ordered. I fumbled ice for him, but he shook that off. "Too cold for rocks. Just leave the straight stuff in."

While he drank, I went back to huffing down the glasses and racking them above the bar. I was aware of the silence, the awkward lag where another person would probably make something of a conversational gambit. The usual members of the bar staff would've known what to do. Debbie might have chatted to him about the snow; Andrea would've flirted; Declan-the-surly would probably have excused himself and draped a towel over his shoulder, then walked around and shuffled the chairs circling the empty tables; while Quinlan would've told a story, all emerald eyes and isles, with a knockout punch-line at the end.

Me, though, plain and simple Jackson Good, I didn't do any of that. I merely stood behind the counter and went about my cleaning. The first trickles of nervous sweat made itches along my back as I polished glasses before racking them, worried my damp skin would be visible through my white shirt before long. I should have worn the vest Quinlan provided for his staff, with the bar's clover emblem on its breast.

"Tell you something, Jackson, if you want to hear it," Mulberry said after the moment of contemplation his drink had engendered in him died away. "It's a crazy world out there, and a man's gotta keep his wits sharp."

"Yes sir, I hear that."

He steered a low laugh in my direction. It sounded mocking to me. "I bet you do. You've not travelled, seen much of the country. I can tell. Been out beyond it, overseas anyplace?"

"No sir. First time in the big city. I'm studying English literature. Thinking of a teaching certificate after."

"You consider you've things to teach people, Mister Jackson Good?"

"Well, maybe not personally, but experience isn't everything. See, what I thought was —"

He pulled me up again, in the same manner he had when I'd listed the drinks for him, with a wide paw of a hand raised in the air. "No, no. I'm gonna stop you there. You need to have *lived* at the edges to be a teacher. A good one anyway. Going straight into a classroom after you've left one, that's no qualification for passing on wisdom. You haven't got any. Except what's come out of the books you've read. And yes, I've no doubt at all that you've read a good few in your time – Mister Dickens and Mister Clemens and all of them – and that you'll read a good few more if you're able. But there's more than book learning, Jackson. What you know in your head, that isn't always the same as what you know in your heart and your guts."

To emphasise his lesson he sank a fist against his chest, which you could imagine rang hollowly, as if there was no heart inside the cage of bones there. Then he patted his paunch. Though his padded lumberjack shirt was not straining at the buttons, it had a steady load to hold in all the same. He was a big man.

"This is where it counts, Jackson. What you *know*, what you feel right down deep in the middle of yourself. Think you can understand some of that?"

"A little."

While I held his gaze, which burned with the fire you sometimes glimpse in the eye of the fanatic, he smiled and stood up. He leaned his weight against the bar top, the heat around his pupils fierce and not blowing out. I didn't know what I should say to him, didn't know what he would say to me next if I didn't speak. I could speculate, suggest he was about to invite me into sharing a little secret knowledge, some random item from his list of cruelties, but I can't be sure. Whatever moment of intimacy we shared fled as quickly as it had appeared. The bar door opened and a rift of wind, harried to a chill by the snow outside, tore across the tables and split the little pocket of the world only Mulberry True and Jackson Good resided within. Fast as a blink, the furnace door over Mulberry's eyes clanged shut and that driven heat in them was gone. The portcullis of his smile likewise disappeared behind his narrow lips.

I looked up to see who'd come in, while Mulberry wiped a hand across his face, turning his palm around on his chin, raising a rasp from a blue patch of stubble he'd missed while shaving that morning.

A bunch of young people walked in, Europeans, I'd say from their accent and dress, leaving the door open longer than Quinlan would have appreciated in such weather. They were laughing and chatting discretely, but their accents carried, a gaggle of boys and girls not much older than I looked. They gained confidence when they saw the bar was empty and they had it all to themselves but for the middle-aged guy who might have been a truck driver and the nervous stick of a barkeep, not too long out of kindergarten and looking like he might be too timid to partake of the strong stuff himself.

Mulberry had a hard time hiding the displeasure he took from their arrival. It twisted his open features into something closed and caged, needful of steel bars to prevent what was inside escaping into the world. He hid himself behind his fingers for a moment. Then he sighed and widened his shoulders in a stretch, placed some notes on the bar counter.

"Think I'll be getting on now," he said. "I can see you've work to be about. I'll catch you later, Jackson. You just be sure to remember what I said. Think about that, how to trust your gut and what it tells you. We have a voice inside that speaks to us. Sometimes it's quiet, sometimes it's not. But you can learn to hear it if you practice hard enough. And you'll learn a lot more if you start to obey what it tells you to do."

Leaving his remaining shot of whisky untouched, he nodded at me solemnly, then slipped his pleasant, unhurried face back into position and made his way into the swirling white blossom of the snow.

When he'd gone, I went to serving the newcomers, and pretty soon the bar busied up with fresh customers and regulars arriving for the lunchtime swell, a buzz of chatter and laughter that ran warmly into the afternoon. I was kept busy enough that I could have been forgiven for forgetting my intense and solitary drinker of earlier. After all, you met plenty of strange guys when you tended bar. But I didn't forget him.

Mulberry was waiting for me outside when my shift was done. I'd been expecting that. He hadn't slipped from my mind during the hours I'd spent serving at Quinlan's, and I was thinking about him as I stepped out into the late afternoon snow.

The streets were covered and cars passed in a respectful, cautious whisper. A chill had already begun moving through the soles of my feet, spreading into my flesh, freezing the crude sticks of bones beneath the maze of stitches on my back, but it didn't concern me. Pedestrians were blurs of wrapped clothing here; no one lingered to watch their breath cloud and catch in front of them. Mulberry had spent the afternoon out in the sub-zero temperatures and he didn't seem to feel a bit of it. A different warmth, that fire I'd seen in his eyes, had kept him ruddy and insulated. His hair was buried beneath flakes, the shoulders of his jacket adrift with them. And yet there was nothing in his aspect to suggest he was troubled by the furies still coming down.

I spied him first, before he registered my arrival on the streets. He looked inhuman for a moment, a thing of inanimate matter waiting to be brought to function. He stood motionless until he saw me, and as if a switch had been flipped somewhere within his brain he jerked into the role of open-faced, nice-to-know-him Mulberry True. It was an act that he was so very good at performing.

"Jackson! Hey, Jackson Good."

He came out of the shadows of the alley where he'd

been standing. There was no logical reason for him having been there, but he didn't seem to notice any lack of surprise on my part. Perhaps it was the Jon-Boy Walton face that I had such a task finding expressions for, or else shards of light had put a cut of reflection to my eyeglasses, concealing the blue irises and their expectation of his arrival.

All the same, I looked around, as if taken aback to see him thrusting forth toward me, so that I might be wondering where he had been holed up and why he was here. "Mister True. What are you doing out here? You haven't been waiting for me, have you?"

He rolled out his laugh and put a hand on my shoulder. "What we were talking about earlier," he said. "Feeling things. From the gut. You been thinking about that? Remember what I told you? That inner voice that talks to you if you listen carefully enough."

I manipulated an expression of confusion. "It's not really . . . I've been busy. The snow, it brings in a lot of people. There's not a lot of time for thinking on things. A day like this, the bar fills up pretty quickly and—"

"I'll bet it does," he interrupted. "But you know, I meant what I said earlier. About how you can't teach unless you know something in your gut, feel it through the beat of your heart. You should understand that. Sometimes it takes a man like me to show people. I feel it's something I need to do. A kind of calling. Bringing that understanding into other people's lives."

If I'd noticed that the cold hadn't affected him, then he didn't appear to have realised its touch made no mark worth acknowledging on me either. We breathed clouds of breath at each other, stood barely moving. I said, "Well, even so, Mister True—"

"Come with me, you've the time." He waved a hand up at a sky grey with fixings of snow. "It's a nothing day. One you can make what you like of."

"Actually, I should be getting back. My studies – there's a lecture . . ."

"They don't matter," he said and propelled me by the force of his big hands in the direction he wanted me to head. "This is what you should do, what you need to learn," he called from behind me, his breath warm in my ear, like a steam locomotive puffing and pushing. I recognised someone in the first grip of a mania. He was striking out on a course and damned if he was going to deviate from it now. "Gonna show you the truth as it is, the real living flesh and blood truth. Experience. Not just words on paper, dates and history. The truth, Jackson. Think of me as a teacher."

"But I don't think I should—"

"C'mon. Face forward or you'll stumble. This'll be good for you, boy."

He hurried me onward, through blurs of falling white flakes, along streets slick and deft with ripples and drifts of slush and snow, a world in transformation, a world dulled of its senses.

In the ordinary way of things, Jackson Good would have wound up in a hundred kinds of hurt that day. Whether those hurts would have been confined only to the physical or else would include insufferable mental deprivations to suffer through, tormented by fierce dreams for the rest of his stricken life, I did not know at that point as Mulberry guided me on. But I was certain Jackson Good would find himself, in one form or another, a different person at the end of the "instruction" Mulberry True wished to carry out.

Mulberry thrust me swiftly through the snow, past steaming vents and along the underside of the overhead rail. He guided me to a rundown area of town, a low life locale, that was all cheap accommodation and grubby living. Trash littered the streets, poking through the snow. Cars were fewer, and the ones we did see were older models running on spit and luck. Whenever I weighted my legs to slow us down they stumbled forward to keep me upright as Mulberry leaned a little of his considerable weight into my back. I was driven resolutely on. There was no stopping him, no escaping him. An arm would loop around me if I tried to take a different direction from the one he wanted me to proceed along, and a fierce band of pain from his grip would crunch my flesh and threaten cartilage or a joint's weakness if I attempted to outpace him.

"Where—?"

"Not far," he said. He seemed to be talking as much to himself as he was to me, or perhaps to a voice he was hearing somewhere inside himself. There was carelessness to his bullying now, the directions he issued coming out bluntly, "left, right, up there," the guiding hands urging me along with considerable acceleration. We were stumbling at a near jog. We nearly missed turns and strode past corners we should have taken in his reckless enthusiasm for what he had planned. We barely saw anyone on the streets, the weather was that foul and turning worse. The snow was coming in curtain after curtain.

"You know," I said. "I really do have somewhere I ought to be. I'm not sure I have the time for this."

"Won't take long," he said distractedly, hustling me into a doorway, beyond which was a short dark corridor with bare wood stairs just visible at the end. He didn't care that he was openly forcing me where he wanted me to go and that anyone we should bump into would be able to see that. In this neighbourhood people had learned the necessity of selective amnesia. "Here, not too far now. Up the flight ahead. I'll show you. Way it works. What's true. A truth from Mulberry True." He laughed skittishly, and I could sense he was not far from hysteria. "I told you my name, right?"

Was he forgetting? In the high drama of what he'd determined to inflict on this poor, clumsy and weak body, was the animal I'd glimpsed in the bar about to come rushing out, overtaking his pretence at humanity? Would it leave him all feral and base? All tooth and claw, wild and unleashed?

I knew that Mulberry True's tally of cruelties was a grim one. And when I'd seen the list, I knew how much fun it would be to meet him. Most souls shrivel like a plastic bag put to a flame at the sight of such horrors. But my soul was long damned and I found nothing to dislike there. I'd been somewhat clumsy taking Jackson for myself, so eager to meet Mulberry. But thankfully the stitches in Jackson's back, crisscrossed together after I'd burrowed into his flesh, hadn't shown through the thin white shirt I wore for the bar work, and Mulberry hadn't seen them, or noticed anything untoward in my character. I was a good impersonator of a simple man. I'm sure he'd appreciate my act, having been so consummate a performer himself for many years. A plain minion of the Downward Place I might be, but my association with Mulberry True would surely escalate me in hiS reptilian eyes, and promotion through the Despicables' ranks would be assured if I could successfully carry out this encounter.

"Through the door, the one at the end of the corridor," Mulberry said, without the first clue to the shock he was about to be subjected to. "You ready for this?"

"Oh, Hell yes," I whispered, ready for him to remove my disguise with knife and drill bit, screwdriver and hammer. I looked around the windowless room he'd prepared. The table with its manacles. The plastic drapes to save blood staining through to the plaster wall and the wood of the floor. The buckets, for the innards. The cleavers and other sharp-edged objects, so neatly aligned on a fold-out decorator's table for his ease.

Just as soon as he'd flailed the flesh from Jackson Good's body, I'd crawl out from beneath the split ribs in my true form, unfurling like a night-blooming orchid, dripping puss and oozing slime, cawing through my beak and curling boned fingernails around his shaking body. Filling the room with my stench, I would show him the truth of what he could become, the deprivations we would share.

Whether my unveiling drove him to the madness that would unleash his blitzkrieg of terror on the world or if he'd have arrived at that state through his own perfectly unnatural means, I did not care. We would be tied together from there on in, ready to commit a multiplicity of outrages. And Mulberry's list of cruelties would lengthen by a thousand new entries.

Not in the slightest bit prepared, Mulberry closed the door. He locked and bolted himself in with me and turned around to look in Jackson Good's eyes, his true face at last revealed.

As he advanced on me, I could almost hear the quill in the Lower Reaches dipping to the ink in anticipation of the many crimes it would come to record after Mulberry finally saw *my* face and our partnership truly began.

lies we tell
the trojans

I once knew a woman who thought the key to happiness lay in the arrangement of the items in your refrigerator. That if the shelf full of tomatoes didn't interfere with the jars of mayonnaise and the beetroot, you'd have a healthy balance mirrored in your life. A kind of *feng shui* of the perishables, if you like.

Lisa Malloy was a kooky girl who wore her hair in dark bangs around vibrant glasses, and when I met her she was working a succession of waitressing jobs in coffee shops and tearooms that housed poetry recitals. I soon learned she read astrology pages and had an idea about becoming something artistic, though she could never settle on whether she wanted to paint, sculpt, play music, or write. She arranged her hair in a new style every week, and when she wore it up she slotted in those sticks at the back of her head, the ones I always think should be used for eating Chinese food.

This woman who communed with fridges and wore

white blouses spotted with big black polka dots and torn jeans went on to become my ex-wife.

I don't want to go into the details of how we came to part, not here, so let's say we argued over the inconsequential things and before we knew it, when we were struck hard, we didn't have anywhere new to go; just more of the same but further on down the lines, destinations darker than ever, lands with overcast skies and no sign of the sun. Maybe the sausages were on the wrong shelf or hadn't been aligned with the poles correctly. Who knows?

I tell you this because I'd been having dinner with a new woman, one of the few truly wonderful experiences left in our lives, stuck as we are between the differing extremes of a world of explosions and secret whispers. It's a relief to sit with someone you hope you're gonna like and to just talk, find out if you have the same sense of humour, whether you're attracted to each other after the initial *ka-boom* of the heart fades. Sometimes it doesn't work out and you find yourself laughing with the guys in the office the next day about how wrong it all went, how you couldn't find a single straight word to say to her, tell them how the lull in the conversation lasted an ice age and you actually saw the wooly mammoth die out. What you don't say is how much it hurts, though, how it feels like another day just got trashed down the dumper and the world got a little darker because of it.

I'd met Rebecca Kyle at a party in the last days of my marriage to Lisa the fridge whisperer, when Lisa and I were officially separated and awaiting the final papers, but still found ourselves attending the same functions because of mutual friends. It had been one of those "hi, how are you?" introductions which never go much further. Rebecca was something in IT and sorted out people's computer programs most the day. The way I remember it, she made magic on websites for companies and navigated her way through lines of electronic code like a bio-chemist plucking at strands of DNA. I do remember liking her a lot, and being struck by how much she reminded me of myself. Her face was my face but with more economy, the squares and angles smoothed out. I think if I'd been a woman, I would have looked very much like Rebecca Kyle.

Call me vain because of that, but I couldn't take my eyes off her that night, and when she and the guy she was with left early, I felt a hollow space at the heart of me, a sinking in my stomach that I'd missed out on something deeply meaningful, maybe even something *spiritual*, whatever that means. I cracked open another bottle and hung out with Jack Daniels after that and the world faded to a blur, as it so often did in those days.

When Rebecca and I bumped into each other on the street – this was more than a year later, after I'd officially split with Lisa and there was only me and Shade and I wasn't drinking so much – it wasn't an opportunity I was going to let slip.

Winter had come in hard, descending on the country like a pack of wild dogs and leaving nothing untouched. Like the preceding days of the week, it had snowed, a good portion of it fractured and transformed to cracked ice on the city streets, scars in a pedestrian war zone or craters on the moon. The world is different under snow, the ordinary shucks away, and you have the sense that anything might happen. I was wearing my usual winter uniform of fingerless gloves and scarf, heavy woollen jacket down to my knees, and I was out taking some air in my lunch hour. Stacked to her nose with shopping bags, Rebecca walked around a blind corner and straight into me.

"Whoa there!"

Her face peeked around the corner of a store bag. "Oh hey, I'm sorry."

It took me a moment to realise what had hit me, and when I did I spoke before she'd chance to gather herself together and skirt around me.

"No, that's okay. Hi. How are you, anyway?"

"Uh?"

She tried to place me, a wary look coming into her eyes because she must get guys coming onto her all the time. As she tried to pin me down she raised an eyebrow and opened her mouth slightly. It was an expression I often felt myself wearing when I was puzzling over something, and I wondered if my smile reminded her of the one she must see bouncing back at her in the mirror each day. Cradling a couple of paper bags with expensive brand names decaled to the fronts, she was wrapped up against the cold in a fawn jacket that had tassels down the arms and fake fur at the ends of the sleeves. She wore tight brown trousers and boots – branded, naturally. Even beneath her light, knitted hat that let stray locks of hair loose she looked good.

"I'm Barney. Barney Kindred. We met at Frank Capron's party last year. You were with some guy with a beard. Drove a BMW and told everyone about it?"

She laughed, and I watched her teeth light her face with even more electricity than had been fizzing there already. Her skin looked healthy in the cold air, out-of-season roses flowering in her cheeks. When she spoke it was with the delight of a schoolgirl discussing a terrible date with the best looking boy in class.

"Oh God! No, don't remind me. I had to listen to him talk about his car all night."

"If it makes you feel any better, so did the rest of us."

"I remember now. It was quite a shindig. There was this little dark-haired woman with loud clothes and a fluorescent Alice-band. She kept running around like she was on fire or something."

I nodded, wearing my I'm-embarrassed-but-it's-true smile. There was really only one way to let her have it.

"Yeah, that was my wife . . ."

"Oh no, I'm sorry." Her hand came up to cover her mouth, though to contain a laugh or hide her embarrassment, I wasn't sure. Having awkwardly transferred the shopping bags under one arm, she now placed them on a dry patch of pavement, possibly the only dry patch, bending down with her knees nicely together and moving in that slinky way only women and cats can manage so gracefully. She was careful with her purchases. Whatever she had in her shopping, it wouldn't be cheap. Rebecca Kyle was not a cheap customer.

"I am really sorry," she said again and stood like a little girl at attention, hands gently folded in front of her jacket, lip quivering as she pretended a frown and looked up at me from under her eyebrows.

"It's okay," I laughed. "And if it makes you feel any better, you're not the only one who was sorry."

"I didn't realise you were married."

"I'm not any more. It, uh, didn't work out – as they say."

"Oh. Okay. So *should* I be apologising?"

I smiled before I'd time to think it over. Some people can twist the world in a word or phrase, show you the view through their eyes so that you're never in quite the same place you were before. Into a land of low clouds and earthquakes, Rebecca had just unfolded a rainbow and slapped it right in the centre of my home. The weight I'd been carrying around somewhere inside lifted and for a moment my head filled with colours. I exhaled a clump of air that had been wrapped around my heart and felt instantly lighter.

"Depends on your point of view, I guess. From here it looks like a good thing."

When she laughed this time she turned her head slightly but kept her eyes on me, the way a puppy will when you play a game with him and he's not sure if you're still fun or not. Breath escaped her wide mouth and was blown away in the east wind, evaporating to the thin sky and mixing with the exhaust fumes of the city traffic. I was suddenly struck by the notion of what it might be like to kiss Rebecca's lips. As I looked into sparkling eyes that were the soft reflections of my own, just for a moment I imagined she'd caught what I was thinking . . .

"Maybe it didn't seem like such a good thing at the time, but it's getting better," I said, feeling the smile still on my face and my cheeks threatening to blush. Both reactions were good, unexpected guests I found I liked staying with me. I hadn't felt like this in years.

"Are you with anyone now, seeing anyone?"

"No, how about you? Still with the guy with the BMW?"

"God no. We broke up and I'm not even sure he noticed. I picture him sitting behind the wheel of his car, an empty seat beside him, trying to work out what's missing. He knows the sat-nav's where it's supposed to be and the rear-window heater's working, there's petrol in the tank and the engine's ticking, but there's something not . . . quite . . . right." She laughed again, a little exasperation, a little resignation there. "Maybe he'll work it out one day."

It turned out she'd been single for nine months, since she'd split with the guy from the party, an astonishingly long time for someone who looked like she did. I remembered the most interesting thing about the guy she'd been seeing was his name: Dylan Ottuno. Maybe I was biased, but I didn't like him. I just couldn't understand what he was doing with a girl like Rebecca in the first place.

"Oh, we weren't together long. It was one of those

things where friends suggested we try it out for a while. I hadn't known him for a week when we went to Frank's party. I'm not really sure what it says about what my friends think of me that they set me up with a guy like Dylan, though. Maybe it's because of how they thought I *should* be?"

"Uh-huh. That can happen. Before I was married, I went on a blind date set up for me by an ex-girlfriend. Disaster from the start. But a fun disaster, if you know what I mean. We were so wrong for each other it was unbelievable. If she said something was black, I'd be convinced it was white, and vice versa. How we didn't end up in a boxing match is beyond me. The thing of it was, my ex-girlfriend genuinely believed we'd be soul mates."

Rebecca smiled, and for the first time since we'd bumped into each other we didn't have anything new to say. The conversation was coming to its natural conclusion, that point where you either shrug and say goodbye or try taking a step further than you thought you were going to a minute before. In a moment she'd leave and that would be the end of that. Unless I bumped into her on another street some time in the future.

"Look," I said, suddenly aware of all the people in heavy jackets dodging by us, the queue of traffic snagging up the street. "I'm just going to get some roasted chestnuts – there's a woman with a little mobile cooker in the square by the church on St Helen's. How about you come join me? I'm in my lunch hour and fancied some air. I could do with a snack. And the company would be nice."

"Roasted chestnuts? God, I haven't had them since I was a little girl."

"Then we'd better change that. You know, the first time I ever had any, I crunched down on the shell as well, didn't eat any more till I was twenty."

"Sophisticated."

"Yeah. I was with my mum and dad, and I remember Dad shaking his head as though it was the kind of thing he'd come to expect of a son of his."

"Do you still eat the shell, because, you know, I don't want to keep embarrassing company?"

"I gave it up. Too fattening. Here, let me take one of your bags."

It was as easy as that.

We must have looked like brother and sister when we sat down to eat an early dinner a couple of evenings later; maybe even twin brother and sister. Our clothes matched and we complimented one another like bookends or hands coming together to make a round of applause. We even ordered the same meal. An extraordinary fact we soon discovered was that we shared not only a birthday but a birth year as well. We were both thirty-six to the day. Maybe even to the hour, for all we could figure. I knew I'd been born late afternoon, and Rebecca actually had the time of her birth – at a quarter to four. As soon as we learned this, Rebecca turned into a nostalgia girl, and for a while the evening went to the tune of "Hey, do you remember . . . ?"

Sometimes it's easy, and it was with Rebecca Kyle – no silences lasting an ice age with her. I didn't even feel like a jerk when she asked me what I did for a living. I told her straight out about selling advertising space in the local press. Didn't even fudge it and try make it sound more glamorous than it quite obviously isn't. For some women, part of a man's mystique lies in his career; what he does with his mind, what he does with his hands, is important. They like to be swept off their feet by the notion that their potential lover is involved in worthy causes – fighting to keep some Brazilian animal sanctuary open, say, or taking disadvantaged kids on canoeing trips through Canada. Lisa married me because I'd been to Art College and had worked for a while making prints of traditional watercolour paints. She seemed to think it was a romantic thing to do, learning the craft before producing masterpieces. It never occurred to her to find out if I actually painted or not. She once said to me, "Barney, do you ever think you'll work again?"

I gave her a nonplussed look. "Uh? What do you mean?"

"I mean get your brushes out, make some canvases up."

The only thing I'd done at Art College was draw; and even then the drawings had been technical pieces, nothing new or representative of anything that wasn't there on a page for me to copy out. Originality's beyond me, something that's somewhere up in the high atmosphere. I've come to realise trauma is an aid to creativity, and it didn't enter my life in any serious way until years after my courses, and by then it was too late to channel the feelings into a different medium. But maybe anything I'd ever had in the way of originality disappeared with alcohol, anyhow.

Lisa was confused and disappointed, but Rebecca took it all easily, and asked me to tell her a story about selling print space. Ordinarily, such stories are only of interest to advertising people or folks who are bored with you but too polite to say so. But I didn't feel that was the case with Rebecca; she was genuinely keen to hear more. So I told her some funny ad tales and then she baffled me with the intricacies of web-design and strange clients who had made fortunes out of sites dedicated to cartoons they watched when they were kids.

We finished up and walked through the lights for a while, shared a cab. I dropped her at her place and rode back home in silence, thinking about how easy it had all been, how I hadn't had to work at anything. Maybe our shared birthday was a sign? For a while I tried to build up a scenario that made it all wrong. But the truth of it was that Rebecca Kyle suited me just fine.

The apartment was in darkness when I got to the top of the stairs (the lift had its usual No Service sign on it) and entered. I was surprised to see it wasn't much after ten. My evening with Rebecca had gone quickly and easily. As I clicked the lights on I noticed Shade on the couch, folding creases in a sheet of old newspaper to make an aeroplane. Scattered pages lay over the cushions around him and he looked like an evil gnome trying to put together a ransom note.

"Hi, Barney."

Shade's four years old, with a high forehead and lips that remind me of his mother. He has my eyes, though. I think when he gets older he'll be slim and athletic. Right now he's an explosion waiting to happen.

"Hi, Shade."

I have custody. Lisa didn't want to know, won't even talk about him the few times we do speak. As far as she's concerned he never existed, was a mistake she has to live with the rest of her life; a bit like me in that respect. There was never any question of him going with her, and even now she doesn't see him. If I so much as try to talk about Shade, it's like a sudden No Entry sign for her at the end of a 40mph zone: she slams on the brakes and slides all over the road, leaving rubber smoking on the asphalt and cops scratching their heads in disbelief. Maybe it's her way of coping with the way her life turned out. Things hadn't gone how she hoped, and she was still picking out shrapnel from the decisions she'd made. Some injuries are deep and never heal, they turn you into a different person, and Lisa was still trying to figure out who she was now. I hadn't looked in her fridge anytime recently, but if I were to make a guess, I'd have said some of the mayonnaise had leaked onto the baby tomatoes.

"Hey there. Whatcha doing, kidda?"

I wasn't all that surprised to find Shade sitting in the dark. You so often finding yourself thinking he's away lost in thought somewhere when all the while he's tapping away at the apartment walls, looking for cracks into the world. There's always something new to entertain him, and if sitting with the lights out making a paper airplane is one of them then it's one of them. I've almost given up being surprised by him. Sometimes he's flighty, prone to sudden mood swings, so the paper aeroplanes were no trouble. He could just as easily have shunned the gloom tonight, stayed away from it and only made an appearance in the light.

"Making stuff."

I watched as he finished folding the plane's nose together, the tip of his tongue sticking out between his lips in concentration. When he was done he smiled, and held his creation up for me to see. Apart from drooping wings too thin to hold it in flight, I thought it was pretty sound.

"Look's good."

"Here!"

He sailed it over towards me and it swooped up and then down in an easy parabola, flapping its wings like a bird as it went, to land softly in a pile of other planes at my feet. They reminded me of the fallen leaves frozen on the paving slabs around the chestnut seller the day I'd bumped into Rebecca and it made me smile. I shook my head, remembering my date this evening, and my heart gave a warm, heavy beat.

"So how's it going, Shade?"

"I watched some TV."

"Yeah? Anything good."

"Cartoons. *Scooby-Doo.*"

A rustle of paper and another airplane sailed my way. It landed by the door as I hung up my jacket. I sloshed through the fallen planes once I'd kicked my shoes off and walked into the kitchen, listening to Shade as he followed and told me about the cartoon.

"So the ghost was actually a person all the time, huh, Shade?"

"Yeah. They always are. Do you think there are real ghosts, Barney?" He hung onto the doorframe, staying away from the cold floor. His socks were trailing halfway off his feet, as if his limbs were melting like the witch in *The Wizard of Oz*.

I popped the top off a carton of milk and sipped from it, wiping away any lingering traces from around my mouth with the back of my hand when I'd done. The interior bulb of the fridge illuminated the kitchen, and as I returned the milk and closed the door the fridge shuddered and the soft kiss of its cold breath vanished. Shadows rushed in and the only light was a diffuse glow, slanting through the blinds. I looked out through the gaps, seeing the city twinkling beyond the distant park in the aftermath of dusk. So many people, so many lives, glimmering in the night. My thoughts seemed stuck a while before I remembered Shade's question and answered softly.

"No. No, I don't believe in ghosts."

But when I turned around he'd already gone.

"Tell me a secret."

Rebecca's breath was close as she pulled herself up my chest, brushed back her hair, and then lowered her head next to mine and moved her lips against my ear in the dark. The warmth accompanying her words sent a shiver through my body, each syllable a phantom passing through my nerves like a summer wind sliding into the back end of October. It was the first time we'd been to bed, and we were naked and still warm from making love. It hadn't been a surprise to find we fit together so well, that where I curved out she curved in, where I was proud she was warm and accommodating. Her breathing was soft and close, and I thought she was as wonderful and dangerous as a lioness beneath the bedding.

I laughed softly, feeling my galloping heart slow some. "I don't think I've any secrets left."

"Mmm," she purred, stroking my chest with her hand. She slid her fingernails over my nipples and I gritted my teeth in delight. She was a girl who liked to tease and she'd been doing plenty of it. "Oh," she said playfully. "Poor baby."

I tensed and she pulled back.

"What? What's wrong? Barney?"

Sitting up perched on one arm, outlined by the light drapes of her bedroom windows, all I could see of her was a silhouette, someone not quite there as the sheets spilled around us, pooling on the bed. I cast my eyes around. No one else was in the room with us, but my ears strained the night just in case. I tried not to panic. My skin was still tender from Rebecca's touch, and I was hypersensitive to the world. Nothing hung in the air, like an echo of a cry after the sharp crack of flesh falling on flesh.

I pushed myself up, heart beating wildly but not in

the happy way it had been a few moments before.

"Barney?"

"I'm okay," I said clasping my arms around my drawn-up knees. "It was nothing." My voice sounded so much louder than the pulse throbbing in my ears. I let go of myself and fumbled for the bedside lamp, the one we'd only turned off a short while back. It flooded the empty room with a yellow glow, and I saw the look in Rebecca's eyes, the frown of concern beneath her tousled hair. She still looked flushed from the sex, but now she was concerned as well. I could see her thinking, *Was it me? Did I do something wrong?*

"Seriously" – I had to speak around a hick in my throat – "it's fine. I'm fine."

"Barney, that's not the kind of reaction a girl expects. You know? Something's wrong. Tell me."

I nodded slowly, closed my eyes. Took a deep breath. "Uh, it's just, this is the first time since I split with Lisa. Officially split with her."

For a moment she didn't know what to say, and then found the words at the end of a breath, all coming out in a rush like she'd been sucker-punched.

"Oh, babes, I'm sorry. I should've realised. I was insensitive. I'm honestly really, really sorry." She reached out, caught between wanting to hold me and not knowing if it was the right thing to do. "Was it bad?" Her brow had furrowed some more in disappointment and concern, and she tossed hair away from her eyes in that gesture she does so automatically that I doubt she's even conscious of it.

"Huh? No. Not at all. God, no. You just said

something she said once, that's all." I shook my head. "It all came flooding back."

"So not good?"

"Bad stuff."

"Sorry."

"Not your fault, honestly."

I lay back down again against the headboard. In such quiet moments of intimacy revelations are so often made. The room seemed both smaller and larger than I knew it was. The pictures hung off the walls awkwardly, the wardrobe looked to be teetering over. Make love to someone and you're sucked into their gravity, the world is only the two of you spun up to a frenzy. Rebecca had ripped a seam out of our air when she'd spoken, and I was only now getting my breath back. I'd imagined . . . but, no. It wasn't the case . . . Everything was okay. I tried to relax and stretched my arm over onto her side of the bed as I calmed down and landed in the real world again, an invitation for her to come join me. She leaned into my embrace, tentatively at first, then snuggling closer and pulling the thin sheet up with her, so that it lay over us, as soft as a spider's web.

"But I am sorry," she eventually said into my chest, her voice reverberating through my flesh and bones.

"Ssh. 'S okay."

After a while I turned off the light, and we lay with only the sounds of our breathing, our bodies' rhythms and beats.

Just before I fell asleep, I thought I heard her whisper something. It sounded like, "No more secrets tonight." And I remember thinking *No, not tonight,* and let unsteady dreams take me.

When I woke it was morning and Shade was swinging from the light fitting. It swayed dangerously from side to side, his weight combining to not only pendulum its motion but to also cause it to spin around first one way, and then, when its momentum had been caught by the twining flex, back the other, giving him a 360 degree view of the room. The bed was empty beside me and I could hear the sound of Rebecca showering elsewhere in the apartment. I was still disoriented from waking up in a different place than usual and I closed my eyes, hoping Shade would go away. But when I opened them he was still there, wearing his red and white pyjamas. Catching the look of disapproval in my eyes, though, he waved to me, blew a succession of comedy kisses, and then . . . vanished.

I got up and made toast and scrambled eggs, my speciality. They were ready and waiting in the little galley kitchen by the time Rebecca was out of the shower. She was wearing towels, a large green one so fluffy you just had to reach out and run your hands over it and the body beneath. The towel's smaller cousin was wrapped around her hair. I was in my trousers, had my unbuttoned shirt on, figuring I'd splash myself with some water by way of a wash later. I'd checked out my socks, but they smelled so bad I'd just balled them and stuffed them in my pocket.

"Oh hey, that's great," Rebecca said, seeing the plate I waved to with a flourish.

"Madame is served."

"She was well served last night." She came closer, lifted her arms and tagged her wrists around the back of my neck and stood on her toes to reach my face. I could smell soap and toothpaste, a newly minted Rebecca. Then, still talking as our lips touched, she said in a muffled sentence that ran into itself, "Ilikedlastnight."

"Mm-hmm? Ilikedittoo."

We broke the kiss, and for a moment as she let go of me and I let her slip out of my hold, I felt as though she'd left a part of herself behind – our auras clinging together, Lisa would have said. I breathed her out and took a new lungful of air, leaned back against the counter as she picked up the plates. "We'll eat out here," she said.

"Okay." I watched her ass move under the towel as she went.

I followed her to a space just inside the balcony doors, where a glass table sat surrounded by three stylish chairs. The chairs and table probably cost more than the whole of my living room furniture added together. She put the plates down, and I placed cutlery next to them as she drew the shutters back and let in the weak morning light. "Back in a sec," she said with a smile and swished off in her towel, returning after a moment with a jug of orange juice and a couple of square glasses. She'd shucked off the smaller towel and her damp hair hung free. I glanced around and was glad to see Shade hadn't made a reappearance anywhere. I figured I'd not see him till later now, when

I left here and headed to work probably.

Because he had a lisp when he was first learning to speak, Shade couldn't pronounce his name properly and instead of the "Adrian" Lisa and I had decided to call him, he could only manage "*Shade*rian". The Shade stuck, though, because I thought it was kind of cute, and he's been that ever since, even though he's grown out of it and can pronounce his words just fine now. It's a natural progression, I suppose. When I first started seeing him I thought I was going crazy, thought that it was an after-effect of coming off the drink and that I was being haunted by my past. I saw the doctor and he had me visit a psychiatric nurse, who put the whole thing in context, said it was actually a healthy way of dealing with the situation and I should just go with it. So I went with it. And here we are.

Rebecca said, "You okay, Barney?"

"Hmm? Sorry. Miles away. I was just thinking on things."

She smiled. "Anything good?"

"Yeah," I lied, and gave her a smile.

Rebecca's apartment was classier than mine. It was located in a better part of the city. Certainly a more exclusive part, one of those area codes you hear mentioned and the only sound you can make is a whistle. She could open her balcony doors and stand outside, look down on nothing but the river and the newly sandblasted stones of the converted warehouse her place was a part of. Compared with my views of the back of the Chinese restaurant and people walking their dogs so they could take a dump on the burned out patch of wasteland before they got to the park, Rebecca's place won hands down.

"Barney . . . Uh, you're sure you're okay with last night?"

"Sure I am. Why'd you ask?"

"You seem a little . . . distant just now."

"Sorry. I didn't mean to be. I had a good time last night, a very good time."

"Hmm. Okay." She put her knife and fork down, wiped her lips with a paper napkin that she'd magicked from someplace, and took some juice. She shrugged.

"What? You don't believe me? I had a good time last night, honestly. Yeah?"

She smiled. "Yes."

"Good. You want anything else? I can do more eggs? Wanna see me crack the shell one-handed? It's a gift."

"Show me some other time," she said still smiling. "Finish up your food. I'll go get dressed."

"You just call if you need a hand."

She laughed and sashayed away, at the last dropping the towel just before she went through the bedroom door and closed it behind her. I waited for her to call me, and when she didn't I shook my head and went back to eating. The juice was good, and I liked the fact you could sit and eat at a window without someone staring at you as they passed by. How do people get to live like this, and why can't we all?

I left for work later than I normally would because Rebecca's pad was nearer the city centre, despite its hush and calm, and I spent the morning with my socks in my pocket and trying not to raise my arms in case I gave off too many noxious odours in the office. At lunchtime I sat shivering on one of the benches by the riverside. It would soon be Christmas, New Year, the usual round of parties, and this time I'd be avoiding any place Lisa and her friends might be. A seizure like panic gripped me when I thought about what might happen if I did run into them.

Shade joined me on the bench as a boat chugged by and the wind played at making icicles out of my hair. He was well wrapped up, and wore big mitten gloves that made his hands look twice the size they should be. Our breathing recorded itself on the air.

"You like her, don't you?"

I nodded.

"So what're you gonna tell her?"

I looked at him, then looked back out across the churned water, partly amazed still that it wasn't frozen over. "I dunno. Maybe I won't tell her anything?"

"I'm gonna be with you the rest of your life, Barney. You know that, don't you?"

"Maybe."

I could get up and leave him behind on the bench, but he might follow. Sometimes it's like that, and he would just remain there; other times he just follows me around. From here I could chase the path, walk to Rebecca's apartment. She wouldn't be there, most likely, unless she was working from home today. But I could do that. I could go see. But what would I say if she was in? We tell lies to ourselves all the time, tell ourselves we look trim in the mirror, that the job's just something we do till something better comes along. We say we could still play sports like we used to when we were kids, if only we wanted to . . . But there are other lies we don't even admit exist, which we readily accept because we don't consciously think about them. How do I feel when I remember the look on Lisa's face? *Don't think about it.* How do I feel when I wake in the dark and it's like her cries have just stopped and the echoes are still hanging in the air, the dead horror of the aftermath of violence? *Don't think about that either.*

Just because you put away the bottle, it doesn't mean you stop living with the consequences of what you've done. There's a tendency to lash out still, to look for reasons, to say "You hurt me, that's why I hurt you"; "You wanted me to hurt you"; "You were looking for it"; "I hit you because you wanted me to, so you could get all you wanted, the power to remind me what I'd done." And maybe I even believe some of that's true, but it still comes down to one thing again: you can't escape the consequences. *Destinations darker than ever.*

"So what are you gonna tell her?"

I turned and looked at Shade, sitting there beside me. His eyes weren't taunting; he wanted the truth. There was concern there, like the look I'd seen in Rebecca's eyes last night when she echoed the words Lisa had cried when she miscarried. In the stark, clinical hospital room, just as her bruises were rising, when I was sober and with her and I still couldn't believe what I'd done.

"Poor baby."

I said, "You're my son, Shade. One day you'll grow up and leave me, or I'll find a way to stop you coming. I can live with you till then. And after? I guess you'll find your own way, in whatever kind of half-life you lead. But Rebecca doesn't need to know. I'm different now . . . I'm a different person. Honestly."

We sat for a while, not speaking, just the two of us, my son and me, on a bench by the river one cold day in winter, though it might look to someone else like a lonely man staring into nothing and trying to find a way to live with himself and what he's done.

working
apprehension

The woman in the smoky grey dress bumped her hip into the rotund gentleman sitting beside her on the backseat of the cab. There was more room now that Walther had got out, here at the corner of Laurel and Collier, and the nudge couldn't be anything but intentional, forcing her fellow passenger to look at her questioningly. Polite Walther had closed the door with a neat clunk, then stepped further back onto the sidewalk. The woman in the smoky grey dress could see him now. He lifted his hat in a wave as the taxi pulled away. His long arm protruded from his shirt cuffs, showing his bony wrist beneath his suit jacket.

"Wave back," the woman instructed, hardly moving her lips from the set expression of her smile.

Her companion, prompted into character, did so. "Yeah, yeah, Walther," he said through the grin of his barred teeth. "Happy happy." It was all faked. "And fuck you very much, too," he said with a sickening, singsong sweetness.

Lexy shifted around, waving through the rear window herself. She watched Walther standing in the bright afternoon, looking so lonely and innocent with his luggage at his feet – until a breeze swept through the sky and the leaves fell like burning snow and the taxi rounded a corner and he was gone. The last she saw of him, he was still smiling and his glasses were bright little coins of sunlight.

Then it was done.

She sighed and turned around to face the front of the cab, folding her hands neatly on her lap. She fingered the fake wedding ring that was already beginning to feel like a stage prop again. She'd lose it soon, along with the costume jewellery necklace. "You know, I'll really miss Walther," she told her companion, the often-insufferable Mr Rexx.

"He was a good one," he agreed, wheezing heavily now that he no longer had a part to play. "If there were more Walthers in the world, our job would be a darn sight easier."

"If there were more Walthers in the world, we might not have jobs," Lexy said. "At least, not these jobs anyway."

Mr Rexx considered this for a moment. When Mr Rexx considers something, he strokes his chin like a ham actor in a Sunday matinee movie. "Say there *were* more of him, a whole world full, everyone nice and naïve, making it a waste of time for us to put our fingers in the pot and stir things up, what do you think you'd do?"

"If we weren't working these assignments?"

"Yes."

"Oh, I don't know." She looked out of her window to the passing scenery, which showed white clapboard houses and picket fences. There were pumpkins on porches already, even though October had barely begun. "I hadn't really thought about it."

"Yes you have. We've all thought about it at one time or another. Can't help but wonder how it'd be if things were different, if we'd never made that choice and signed up for this."

"I suppose you're right."

Mr Rexx grunted. He unwrapped a cigar and chewed on it, though he resisted the urge to strike a match and start smoking. He'd save that for nearer the airport. It was just his way. "So what is it? What'd you do? Seriously. If we weren't in this game?"

Lexy stretched her legs, slipping her feet out of her heels. She pushed back into the seat and flashed Mr Rexx a shy smile, as if about to confess a secret. "I'd live in Denver and I'd be married, maybe to a junior high school teacher. Though for a while before I met him I'd've been an airhostess and have had wonderful affairs and I'd know how to speak French."

Mr Rexx laughed at that – a congested laugh, which could complicate into a throaty expulsion of wet mucus if he wasn't careful. It wasn't an attractive feature, and he had to rein in his expressions of mirth when they were on the job; it didn't do to let the mark see such a slip, the rot beneath the presentable facade. The ugly beneath the happy.

"You think that's funny?" Lexy said.

He waved one of his meaty hands at her. After he'd taken his unlit cigar from his mouth and patted his lips with a handkerchief, he told her, "Shucks no. A honey like you, you'd be perfectly suited to the job."

"Then why the laughter?"

"I thought you were going to say something else, like you'd imagined yourself starring in the pictures. A modern-day Veronica Lake, something like that." He shook his head. "An airhostess, that's not what I'd have expected. There's not enough ambition in that, I guess. I thought you'd want more out of life."

"No," she said quietly, turning once more to look out the window. "Not any more."

A boy on a bicycle was pedalling as fast as he could beside the cab, pulling bumps on the sidewalk and standing tall as he went. His hair – too long, Lexy thought, he needs to get it cut – sprayed out behind him and bounced when he crossed flagstones that heavy cars had buckled to dips and launch pads over years of pulling into their driveways. He was enjoying himself, unaware of how glad he was to be alive. When the taxi turned right the boy skewed his handlebars to one side and spun his rear wheel around in a half moon, so that he was facing the way he'd come. After a fragment of a pause he began pedalling back, spokes silvered to a whirl. Lexy watched until she couldn't see him any more.

"What about you?" she said, turning away from the world beyond the cab and the life she'd never know. "If there were more Walthers out there, if everyone on the planet was as nice as him, what would you do?"

Mr Rexx twisted his lips dismissively, as if such matters were not really his concern or worth his time considering for very long. He'd put away his unlighted cigar, having tasted enough, and was massaging his knuckles. "Mmm," he said. "Something or other."

"You must have an idea," Lexy said. "You just told me everyone in our line thinks about it sometimes."

"Maybe I'm the exception."

"I don't believe so."

He mulled on that for a moment, before confessing, "No. You're right."

But he still didn't offer an answer.

There sat between them the sounds of the taxi for a while, the purr and mutter of the engine, the whine of acceleration and a slight rumble of the brakes catching when they slowed. They'd crossed into downtown and passed the courthouse, were now going by the mall and already there were signs indicating the route they would follow out to the freeway. "So, seriously – what is it?" Lexy asked eventually. "What would you do if we weren't working for the Apprehension?"

Mr Rexx breathed deeply. Air entered his congested passages as if it were reluctant to do so. He let it bubble out of his mouth, a sound that made Lexy think of a clown deflating. As ever, she hid her distaste of him. "I thought I might write," he said.

It was Lexy's turn to be surprised. "As in a *book*," she said.

"Sure a book. Why not?"

"But . . ."

"But what?"

"But I've never seen you reading anything. You toss the paper aside after five minutes. I've only ever seen you glance through the sports spreads."

He shrugged. "I didn't say it was a practical thing, something I was *going* to do. Just what I'd like to do if I had the choice. Like with you being an airhostess, as serious as that. Anyhow, you see those famous writers and it doesn't look so hard. Once you got your story, it's just a question of knowing where you put the dots and squiggles. You've got all the words already. And you know something else, those writers, they got people called editors who fix most of that for them, the technical stuff."

She was about to say more, but didn't get the chance.

"Hush up a minute," Mr Rexx told her out of the side of his mouth. He leaned forward and tapped on the partition to the driver. When the driver slid the glass back, Mr Rexx said, "When we're out of town again, just before we get onto the freeway, I want you to pull up by the bridge. You know the one I mean, runs over the Wilmington?"

"I know the one," the cabby said. The light strains of swing tunes were playing from his radio.

"Pull up there."

Mr Rexx slid the partition back into place, muting Benny Goodman's clarinet, and settled back in his seat, glancing at Lexy. She said nothing; she was familiair wih all of what came next. It was standard procedure. She nodded to show she understood. From the accordion business case by his feet, Mr Rexx extracted a brown paper bag. It was unused and in pristine condition, folded as if it had been ironed. Lexy was aware that Mr Rexx was a fastidious man and that there was a decent possibility that the bag *had* been ironed; he'd have done it back at the hotel. Mr Rexx was particular about such things, despite his own tendency to look shabby even when he was playing a role.

"You know the list?" he said. "Want me to read it you?"

"Necklace, ring," she recited, itemising a few more things from memory before finishing with, "Do I really have to give up the watch, though?"

He nodded, eyes flat and unmoving.

"But I really like this watch. See the face – look, you can see it has a pearl in it. A tiny one, it's true. But it's a pearl, all the same. I never had a watch with a pearl in it before. No one would ever know if I kept it."

He only had to say her name.

"I know, I know," she said resignedly, and undid the strap from her wrist. The watch went into the brown paper bag along with the necklace and the plain band of the bogus wedding ring, the keys and her bangles, all the paper items from her purse, her mocked-up ID, and a hairpin. After this, Mr Rexx added his heavy watch and copper bracelet. He shifted his weight and removed his wallet from his rear pocket, took out his billfold and loose change and put them in his pocket. The documents he left inside the wallet, which he dropped in the bag after the other items and then made origami of the checklist and included that, too.

"It's everything," he said.

He bunched up the bag's neck, like the cellophane wrap around a toffee apple you buy over a counter at the county fair, and clenched his fist around it.

Lexy stayed silent and looked at her feet, homing in on the toes at the end of her stockings, counting them all the way to ten. She felt as if she had deposited another life into the contents of yet another disposable brown paper bag. How many was it now? Enough that she'd lost count. This one wasn't the life of a retired airhostess living in Denver, but it might have been for all that the act of disposing of it represented to her.

"Lexy."

She glanced up to see her companion studying her, as if he'd asked her a question and she'd not replied. The empty space where words should have fitted gaped between her lips and for a moment she grew scared, worried she'd done something wrong. Mr Rexx made slits of his eyes, studying her, and then frowned. He shook his head and put himself into action, bulldozing his shoulders and then the rest of his body into motion.

"Won't be a moment," he said, and she realised they were no longer in motion. The taxi had pulled over. She'd been too busy considering her loss, and then frightened by the way he'd appraised her, to notice they weren't moving any more. When she looked out the window, she saw that they were beyond the suburbs, the town long since left behind, and were parked on the quiet, leafy road before the fast straight run to the freeway and the airport. Mr Rexx opened his door and fresh country air hustled its way in while he climbed out.

Alone in the back of the cab, Lexy released her anxiety on a frayed string of breath and watched him march squarely away from the roadside, moving into the bushes alongside the end of the bridge. He wouldn't have hurt her, not in the back of the cab, not so openly, she thought. But he could do later if he thought she was wavering. Lexy kept an eye on where he had disappeared. She might have caught sight of the bag rising and falling in a parabola through the air, but it was so swift she couldn't be sure. She'd seen nothing more concrete than a shadow; it might have been a bird, disturbed by Mr Rexx as he pushed through the brush. But she didn't think so. Not many seconds after that Mr Rexx was back, breathing heavily, smelling as if his clothes had been hung out to dry on a line. He closed the door behind him, with a heavier clunk than Walther had done when he'd got out – poor Walther, neat, pristine and good-hearted Walther – and spread onto the seat.

"Drive," Mr Rexx said, mouthing the words exaggeratedly as he tapped on the partition. There was no need to slide it back. The cabbie understood, and slipped into gear and drove them out of there, quickly crossing the bridge.

They were leaving behind a fast-flowing tidal river. Mr Rexx had checked it out a few days before, Lexy knew, when everything with Walther was building to a finale. The paper bag would float downstream a while, before it dissolved in the water, spreading its contents over a good stretch of the river. Should the authorities bother to dredge the bottom to look for any sign of them, over such a distance it was unlikely the costume items would ever be found. Even if they were, they'd be of no real value to the police. Just something else to confound them.

When the taxi hit the on ramp and joined the flow of traffic moving south, Mr Rexx perceptibly relaxed.

"Another one done," he said. "We'll be away pretty soon, flying. You can forget all about it now, sweets. You did good on this one. For a while I thought you were getting too close to the mark, becoming emotionally involved. But you were great." He nodded to demonstrate he was satisfied with her performance, and he hung his cigar back on a lip, shook a box of matches in his hand. "It's important to keep them at a distance. There'll be another client to think about when we get back to the offices. A new assignment. There's always a new assignment."

As Mr Rexx wound his window down and struck a light and got his cigar going, Lexy closed her eyes, trying not to focus her thoughts on Walther and what they'd done to him. But he was a hard guy to forget. Would he have realised yet, she wondered? Or had he not worked out that he'd been taken for everything but the few possessions he had in that forlorn-looking suitcase? She reassured herself that he'd be fine. People like Walther always were. They took the knocks, bowed and bent like the tree that survives the storm. Without him and his kind, the world would be one of uprooted old oaks, their arthritic roots knotting over the face of the earth. There'd be no high bows and leafy crowns for the great birds to nest in, nor dappled sunlight making freckled shadows on the green grass of meadows spread for picnics. Walther would be okay. Shaken and sullen for a while, his trust in the goodness of human nature hurt maybe, his faith slightly corroded – it was only the first step, a little victory, but an important one for the Apprehension – but ultimately he'd survive.

All the same, Lexy hated that she had to bring unhappiness into his life. But it was what she'd signed up for when she'd joined the Apprehension. Hurting Walther and people like him. All the little Walthers of the world, happy and contented, until she came along. She'd been young. No excuse. Just a fact. That painful twist of kink in her had wanted to bring chaos to people who were as inoffensive as you could get and had never hurt anyone. It had taken shamefully little persuasion from Mr Rexx to get her to write her name on the contract. He'd seen the potential she had for cruelty, and had known just how to encourage her.

Now it hurt to be doing this and she knew there was no way out. Some contracts you signed with more than blood . . .

The car drove, the tyres hummed, the road went on, and her heart felt the pain that comes from an illness of the soul.

"Mr Rexx," she said, recognising the empty void within herself and not wanting to face it.

"Yes?"

"Wake me when we get close to the airport. You

know I like to watch the planes come in to land."

Not waiting to hear his reply, she lifted her feet and curled her legs on the seat, resting her head into the corner where the backrest met the wall of the cab. She was careful to keep her face turned away from her companion, so that he wouldn't notice any tears if they came. She could be alone with her thoughts and her unhappiness now, if only for a while.

the symphony
of frogs

People enter and leave our lives so often that it's impossible for us to keep track of them all. A few of them stay a while, weave some vital essence of themselves into the fabric of our days, and only unstitch their threads with long, slow strokes, disappearing in increments without you realising they have done so. Until one day they are simply gone and all that lies in their place is the seam they once wove, now frayed and sagging in their absence. And with dawning comprehension of their departure, you wonder how they ever left so quietly, and, in their going, went unnoticed for so long. But as true as this is, I have also found that there are those whose touch lingers long after their physical presence has departed. It is as if a part of you is for ever changed by having met them, and, like the long trailing strands of gossamer that spiders unspool on the breeze in the hope of ensnaring a fly, they snag you and cling to you and never entirely let you go.

The German market came to the city just before Christmas, setting its stalls and kiosks out under awnings that flapped with the cold wind blowing off the ring road into Millennium Square. It was a chilling, semi-arctic blast that swooped in over the country and sent the red-faced crowds ducking into the low-roofed temporary drinks hostelry that had been constructed in the lee of an old building that went up during the industrial revolution. The hostelry was on wheels, an unfolded container from the back of a lorry, and had been stylised with large sheets of timber painted to look wildwood rustic. There were even braziers inside, which added to the gloom of the smoky interior, dulling it further and leaving an aroma of wood smoke that danced languidly in the air, mixing with the sweet scent of cigarettes and something vaguely foreign. But for all that it offered some respite from the cold, few lingered inside for very long.

By the start of the next year, an ice rink would be standing on the same spot in the square and brightly coloured skaters circling it with varying degrees of skill, until the softer days of March arrived, when a roller-blade arcade would replace it and pump out disco hits through loudspeakers for a few weeks. Built, not all that surprisingly given its name, for the recent year 2000 celebrations, the square's primary use was to accommodate whatever passing fancy came the city's way. Crowds had watched various successes and failures of the national and local sports teams on vast TV screens there; rock concerts by artists of varying popularity had been held in the square; and even the occasional orchestral recital had taken place when the area wasn't in use for something more high octane.

But we had no idea the square had undergone another of its transformations when we drove into the city that December day. As far as we were concerned it was just another Sunday, probably the last before the Christmas rush began, a final chance to avoid being jostled off the streets by shoppers as they dashed around in search of commercial fulfilment – *See, darling, I love you because I spent my weekly income on you.*

Our plans went no further than walking around the bookstores and taking espressos in a coffee house before tiredness prevented us doing any more. After that, we'd wander back to the car and drive home, congratulating ourselves on a day without incident. The kind of thing a normal couple would take for granted. (And it should be said that if you were to see us on the street, you'd think we were just another couple; there wasn't anything you could point to, nothing to single us out and allow you to say we were different. We didn't wear our marks that easily. They lay deep inside, somewhere where the codes of our being resided, beyond the ability of medical ingenuity to unravel and smooth over.)

When the scents and sounds of the market drifted to us, we paused. Francesca tugged on me and steered us towards the square, in the direction of the colourful banners we saw rippling loudly and brightly like streamers blown by clowns. Something different was there, a new and unexpected change in the air, like a sudden heady scent of blossom in autumn. We smiled at each other in hopeful anticipation, daring to share the same thoughts but not quite brave enough to say them in case they melted on our tongues. We couldn't help think it, though, and wondered if one of our surprise gift boxes lay waiting to be opened.

Our luck so often went that way, and although we never questioned it, we delighted in the small pleasures presented by our being together and stumbling upon an unexpected foreign market or a street trail of ice sculptures. We had been unlucky in so many other respects it seemed only fair that there should be a balancing of the scales somewhere along the way. And for us that balance lay in moments of discovery like this.

"Looks like a fair of some sort," I remember saying as I noted the wooden roofed kiosks and canvas awnings set up in a rough collection of avenues and lanes. The square had room enough to accommodate this temporary village without too much difficulty, and even had space leftover for a couple of fairground rides at the edges. Above everything, over the discordant clash of organ tunes and calliope music and chilled laughter and the cries of children, flags flapped and ripped at a pale sky that seemed almost transluscent. There was no snow, but if it fell it would hardly be a surprise. I've come to think that winter skies are thinner than summer ones. It's as if the planet's atmosphere weakens until the sun returns and it can stretch out in something like freedom once more. Such a sky spread over us on that Sunday, and sometimes, even when I am standing in the brightest sunlight on the warmest of days, surrounded by my garden in its full summer pomp, I think its chill has never entirely left me.

"Is it French, Tom? Or maybe it's that Swedish one?"

I shook my head slowly, working the muscles in my neck as Francesca cuddled into me. I'd put a scarf on that morning and was beginning to suspect it had been a mistake. It might keep me warm, but it was constricting, making me stiffen and ache there, and I had aches enough already without adding to their number. I considered taking it off, but was content for the moment to let Francesca guide me in the direction of the people and the stalls. I could stuff it in my jacket pocket later, relish its removal when the wind wasn't as harsh. As it was, I don't recall when I did eventually lose it. By then so much else was happening that removing the scarf was something I hardly took note of.

"I think the Swedish one will be in another part of the country by now, Fran."

I remembered the last market we'd stumbled upon just a month ago, in the small town nearer to home. We'd shared a ration of lemon pancakes, sprinkled with a light coating of white powder, and the pancakes steamed in the cold air as we fed each other hand to mouth. It is one of my most treasured memories.

As she leaned into me as we approached the square, I kissed Francesca on the top of her head, where the part of her hair revealed a thin line of pale skin beneath. My Snow White. She looked up at me and smiled.

"So what do we think this one is, then?"

"Let's find out."

As we drew closer, the provenance of the fair became more obvious. Big frau tanks with bosoms like atom bombs manoeuvred their way behind the stall counters, and thinner pale-skinned blondes with dark marks under their eyes filled bags of fudge or ginger for customers in exchange for a currency they were unfamiliar with and struggled to negotiate change for. We smiled as big men with moustaches and prodigious paunches nodded approvingly from behind tills and grinned and spoke to each other in their own language as they sold wooden ducks and knick-knacks, or else ladled out generous helpings of thick broths into polystyrene dishes you were expected to eat out of with plastic spoons. All that was missing was an oompa band dressed in lederhosen; and in that regard we had to settle for differing varieties of organ music playing from stall to stall, each one trying to outdo the calliope sounds from the rides.

"It's German." I pointed to a banner we'd missed. It was strung overhead, and had twisted and folded around itself; it'd been whipped that way by the wind, making the words hard to read. "There's a sign says so. Traditional, as well. Want a wander round, chestnut?"

Of course, I knew the answer before I asked. But how I wish now that I'd been mistaken.

✻   ✻   ✻

She came to me again in the night, when my mind and body were at their weakest. It was not the first time I had dreamed her thus, sharing my bed, filling the depression in the old mattress we had for so long debated about replacing. But she was there, if only briefly. The moonlight might have played with my perceptions, it's true; or it might simply be that in my half-conscious state I misinterpreted what I thought I heard and felt. But she was there; in any way that matters, she was there. I'll swear to that.

Once I had lost her and knew so without doubt, I left the mattress as it was, the argument about replacing it over and done with, with no one to play its cadences against. In truth, I thought it unlikely I would ever replace it. Long years might pass, springs erupt from the bedding, stuffing spread forth, and all manner of crawling life inhabit it, but I did not truly think it would come to be exchanged for another. I saw myself projected into the future, in this same grey room, the furnishing years out of date and covered with dust, a tired old man, body aching but now with the ravages of time, and I would be lying there at my last, until whoever found me took me away forever, to be boxed and sunk beneath the sod, a stone marker planted over my head with names and dates that meant nothing to anyone chiselled deep in its face. And still the mattress we had shared, however old and torn, sagging and uncomfortable, would be there as they removed me, her presence still delineated in its whorls and ridges, unique as any fingerprint to its owner, its possessor. A mark that said I was here. A mark that lingered, would not let go.

But for a moment in the night, on our mattress where we had so often lain together coupled in sweet soft rapture, she was there, and I was not an old man but a young one in all kinds of pain, and the weight on her side of the bed and the feel of another beside me could not be denied.

Beyond the pumping of blood in my ears I heard the breath of another, one so familiar as the slight whistle of air through her nose sang its sleepy lullaby. And when I reached behind me with trembling hands it was to lay my fingers on her cold back, and feel the movement of her sharp ribs rising and falling beneath the thin material that covered them. If something fluttered there, a buzzing presence, it should not feel like a moth's racing wings but a heartbeat, or a soul within skin and bone, aching for release.

How long did we stay that way? No time at all. It could only have been seconds; certainly it was less than a minute. I remember the beating in my chest, remember every part of myself being so alive knowing she was there, back with me. And in the night, in a dark leavened of its edge by moonlight, I was scared. The house stretched around me, larger than it should be, an empty shell with its windows fastened, its doors locked. No one should be there with me. Whatever I shared the house with, I shared it alone.

When I finally gathered my courage and turned over to look upon her, she was gone. Only the cold she had left where she had lain remained, as the bedding deflated and fell. I watched it curl inward, like autumn leaves, sighing in to the mattress, pale and forgotten in the ambient light the moon cast beyond the branches of the willow outside the bedroom window.

A dream, it is entirely possible to reason. It must have been. The dead do not return; it would have been in the news had it been the case. There would be documents pertaining to the fact, articles in magazines, discourses on the subject broadcast on television and radio. There have been no such writings, no such programmes.

But she was there. She was.

The next day I opened the evening paper and read a report about a rain of frogs in the village. They had fallen at midday, out of a perfectly blue sky as a wedding party left the church, congregating in the graveyard. The frogs that survived the downpour made their way over their dead cousins to the stream beyond the boundaries of the churchyard. The frogs that had perished with the fall lay there to be photographed later, with the confused vicar stooping over them, a puzzled smile on his face.

Though I did not know around whose grave the frogs fell, I could guess. I did not need to visit the churchyard to find out. Nor could I have asked for better confirmation of the reality of my nighttime visitor.

*   *   *

Ours was a sedate life. Our illnesses ensured it was so. Since childhood we had each been tainted by the same affliction, and I can say now that if all of the years I spent in pain resulted only in my meeting Francesca and nothing more, then the pain was a small price, the charge ridiculously low. We had our ways. We didn't rush, and were careful to plan our hours according to our limitations. Our days consisted of balancing acts of activity and rest, trying not to exceed what we were capable of, making sure we didn't leave ourselves exhausted and fatigued by the result.

We were careful, as I say. We had to be. How ironic that we were so in all the ways but the most necessary.

These small trips of ours were one of our few luxuries, and we valued them so much. It was why finding the market had seemed such a wonderful thing, one of those pearls we extracted from the damaged shells of our lives and pored over, delighting in its gleam.

And so we had our time in the market.

"Oh my God, look at those! Aren't they cute?"

I laughed when I saw what Francesca was pointing at. A stall heaving with wooden carvings of various animals had attracted a large crowd, and she had spotted a gap, pulled me after her to protect her as she stood at the front of the display. Strange animal sounds that were not quite alive had been calling from over the heads of the crowd, louder even than the ratchet clicks of the amusement rides and the oompa music, and we had peered this way trying to find their origin. Now we understood.

"See the owl, he make the sound," a young woman said and demonstrated. She held a carved effigy of an owl about the size of her fist before her, and put her lips to the back of its head. Blowing into an aperture there, she produced a sound from the hollow under its beak that I had to admit was convincingly owl-like. She put it down, nodded, and selected another animal, an elephant, this time, and demonstrated that one by humming a note through its back. The crowd applauded as a fair imitation of a wild *trumpet* came from its trunk. Smiling, the girl broke off to serve someone, promising more in a moment.

As the girl was busy packing away an owl, Francesca and I looked at the other carvings, which were stacked shelf after shelf on the high counter. There were numerous creatures of varying shapes and sizes, all carved from a reddish wood, all of which seemed in one manner or another to be designed to make a noise.

"You want one?"

She nodded. "Shall we?"

"Sure, they're not all that expensive. What do you think, a giraffe?"

"There is no giraffe!"

"Well, there ought to be."

"Oh yeah? And what sort of noise would they make?"

"Some sort of munching sound when they eat leaves, I guess." But the matter of which creature to choose was quickly settled when the girl returned to her demonstration and pulled a large, dark, wooden frog from the wall. It was the size of a cat and its back had a set of ridges carved into it, and in a round hollow behind the slit of its mouth it held a baton like a miniature Louisville slugger. We watched as the slugger was removed and the girl ran it carefully up and down the ridges on the frog's back, making a reverberation that with a little moderation sounded like a frog croaking.

The crowd began to clap and the girl nodded her acknowledgment.

"Think she can make it say *Bud-Weis-Er*?" I whispered to Francesca.

She tapped me playfully on the arm.

"I want a frog, Tom."

I smiled and nodded. "Let's see what they've got."

We found some the size of our palms, and when we noticed a little sign pinned to a strut holding the stall roof up telling the story behind the construction of the frog we decided we needed two. I paid the lady and she gave us a couple of photocopied pieces of paper inside the pair of plastic bags she wrapped the frogs in.

Francesca smiled and said "Now we can never lose each other" and we slid out of the crowd that was pushing in on the stall, departing to the notes being played on the back of the large frog. *Croak, croak, croak.* As the sounds of the wooden creatures were lost and mingled in the fog of market noises, Francesca stood on tiptoe to give me a kiss, a soft dry brushing of lips. She sighed, happy. "Thank you, you."

"You're welcome. For what?"

"For being you. For finding me."

I hugged her, pulling her close, and didn't stop until she giggled and laughed and complained I was crushing her. "Stop it! Let go, you idiot." When I released her it was to find her fingers laced with mine, one of those tricks she could pull that I never really figured the method of but which I liked all the same. It was a sort of magic; the best kind I've ever known. I dabbed her on the nose.

"We found each other, Francesca Ogilvy. Would've done so no matter what, whatever was in our way."

She nodded, and I could see her thinking of the years illness had stolen from us. I felt her swift depression descend like a heavy cloud. Suddenly the whirl of all that missing time we had lost to our maladies spun around us. Or maybe it was just the wind – you can hope as much sometimes – blowing sharp brittle fragments that puncture your heart, like a litter of leaves coming loose from a forest tumbled all the way into a lost season.

"C'mon, Tom," she sighed. "Let's see what else there is."

We stall-shopped, which I guess is the equivalent of window-shopping, hanging back behind other customers and just murmuring about the nick-knacks and gee-gaws we saw glittering on display, many of which were available in stores in the city centre for a fraction of the cost. We weren't entirely invisible to the stallholders, though, and found ourselves talked into sharing a hot banana coated with chocolate, skewered lengthwise on something that looked like a kebab stick. "Give you plenty energy; pound two, please" the rather intimidating stallholder told us. We paid up before he called in the German equivalent of the mafia on us, and walked off to try figure out how you ate a chocolate-coated banana on a sharp stick without impaling yourself.

I was beginning to feel the cold again, and I knew I would be looking drained. It wasn't long before Francesca saw as much.

"Sit down, Tom?"

I nodded, and we left the hubbub of the thickening crowd and found a bench by the fake German hostelry. We'd looked in on the hostelry, but the smell and gloom had been enough to put us off, despite its promise of some warmth and respite from the wind. The scent of decay from a nearby rubbish bin wasn't too enticing as we took our seats, and when Francesca declined my offer she should finish the banana I flipped what was left in the bin. We remained sitting on the bench, not speaking for a while, and I tried not to think about the pain in my feet or the sharp stings in my joints. My hands felt swollen and the scarf was giving me a bad crick in the neck. But I wanted to know how Francesca was doing.

"You okay?"

"Uh huh. Just got a bit breathless. I'll be okay in a sec."

I put my arm around her shoulders and she leaned into me. I felt the ache in my neck spread down my back, twitching my muscles and weighing heavily there. But I let it go. It would only make Francesca unhappy if I pulled the scarf off. It would draw attention to the fact I was hurting as well. We'd only just arrived in the town really, and there was plenty of day ahead of us. Depressing to have to contemplate it, but we'd take rests like this as we went to make things easier.

We stayed where we were for a little while, just being quiet, just having a moment to ourselves.

Perhaps that was when he first saw us.

I returned to Lily Pond Cottage in darkness, refusing the offer of a bed at my parents'. My father had my brother drive him over to the city to bring the car and me back after all the stuff with the police was done. Or at least, I should probably say, after all the stuff with the police had come to rest with something like equilibrium . . . for now. I wasn't in a fit enough state to drive. I said nothing that I remember on the journey home, though I know we must have spoken. My father is not the kind of man to keep silences, and his frustration at the day's events must have poured out of him like water down the babbling little fall that leads to the graveyard pond from which the cottage takes its name. There would be sympathy, of course, mixed with the phrasing of his sentences that suggested I was in some way to blame for what had happened.

I assured him that I wanted dropping off at the cottage – the end building in a row of terrace cottages that my brother had redeveloped in the last few years and which Francesca and I took at a reduced rent. I wanted to be near the phone in case the police called (this was in the days before mobile phones were as ubiquitous as they are today). But already I knew I had lost her and that when the call came it would not be to tell me anything I wanted to hear. All that was left was uncertainty and then after that would come the rituals.

The house echoed with emptiness as I closed the door behind me, and when I saw the space on the rack beside the other coats I understood at once that everywhere I went would be haunted now. For a moment I could not move, and it seemed as if reality were holding itself still. Then the ticking of the clock resumed, and in the universe's new motion I unbuttoned my coat though I did not take it off. I moved away from the open staircase and into the living room, feeling hemmed in by the thick stone walls and the narrow exposed ceiling beams, and then I turned around and threw myself at the coats. I buried my face in Francesca's other jackets, inhaling as deeply as I could, gulping down the scent of my lost girl.

Her presence filled my head, it circulated in my lungs. And with each exhalation she was a little more gone.

When I lost the strength to stand, I slid down, bawling, holding onto the hem of her clothes. When the shudders that gripped me let go, I moved away from the coats, letting them trail from my fingers as an enormous tiredness overcame me. I ached so very much. Ached and ached. Utterly spent, I folded myself onto the old sofa and wondered what I would do now. And yet the thought of doing anything was absurd. I could only stay here, for ever and ever.

The room was quiet but for the ticking of the clock on the mantle, an heirloom of Francesca's, and the noise seemed unnaturally loud. It challenged the beat of my heart. It unnerved me, for all the numbness I was feeling.

Stiff and unwieldy, I reached into my bulging coat pockets, knowing I would not sleep upstairs tonight, that I would have to get comfortable where I was now, that I was too tired – physically and emotionally – to do any more. But the expected scarf wasn't there. Instead I pulled out a clear plastic bag, seeing the dark wooden frog inside, with its miniature Louiseville slugger tucked away in its mouth.

She must not have come that first night, but then I had not really tried to summon her. Not properly. Not in the way I should have done. As I lay on the couch, drifting in and out of sleep, I did not hear the floorboards creak above me, the sounds of the bedsprings strain under her hollow weight. If the bed were somehow colder in the morning when I went upstairs, floating almost aimlessly, it must be because damp had crept in beneath the sheets. I might have dreamed other sounds that night, but when I awoke it was to see the embers in the fireplace slowly dimming and I knew I was alone in the house and panic rushed over me.

The police called me that morning, as I knew at some

point in time they would. They had found her. A man had been arrested.

"Here, I need to go."

"Huh?"

She handed me her bag.

"Hold onto this, I won't be a moment. I hope there's not a queue or anything."

She nodded at the portable toilets and I expressed my understanding.

"Ah. Okay. I'll just be over here, yeah? Have a nice evacuation."

"Idiot."

I watched her walk off, wiggling her fingers at me in a wave. She held her frog up in its plastic bag and made a "call me" sign by bringing her little finger and thumb up to the side of her head and I waved back at her, mouthing "*Bud-Weis-Er*" and pretending to raise a can to my lips. As she waited in the short line of women standing before the cubicle door, I turned my attention to the sounds from the amusement ride, a Grimms' Fairy Tale attraction. Motorised carriages whipped up and down along an ingenious track that took advantage of the limited space, rushing into dips and clattering up inclines to drop swiftly down again below representations of fairies and wicked witches . . . and grey, yellow-eyed wolves.

I dipped a hand into my pocket and pulled out the soundfrog, opened up the plastic bag and took out the little sheet of paper. It recounted the same story as the sign on the side of the stall.

Once upon a time in a continent called Asia, a young prince and his forbidden love agreed to meet beneath the Banyan tree at the edge of a dangerous moor. When one of them stood beneath the other's window and played the soundfrog *and the other reciprocated by playing their* soundfrog, *that would be the signal to meet later that night. The* soundfrogs *duly sang and the prince and his love left for the moors. As both hastened to the assignation, a deep mist fell on the land and the lovers became lost on the tricky moor and were never seen again. From that day forth, when a thick mist steals all detail from the world, their ghosts can be heard calling on the frogs as they try to find each other.*

Well, there's a happy little tale, I thought, and smiling put the paper back in with the frog, tied the wrap on the plastic bag, dropped it in my coat pocket and watched the kids' faces as they swooped around the inclines on the Fairy Tale ride. They whooped and shouted, enjoying their safe scares and timed thrills. Oh to live with such sanctioned fear.

I leaned there on the railings as I waited for Francesca to return, her handbag hanging off my shoulder. As I did so, I paid no attention to the people passing behind me, any one of whom could have been him.

The path from the back of the cottage leads to an old bare wooden gate going grey with sunlight. It hangs unevenly and, when opened or closed, squeals on hinges that are peppery with rust. In moonlight, however, the gate gleams palely and the stone flags lining the path shimmer, as cold as stepping-stones across a stagnant pond. At night, of late, I often find myself walking to it and stand there barefoot. I rest my forearms on the rough wooden grain, getting my breath back and reflecting on how much worse my malady has become since I've been alone.

I look out ahead, beyond the gate. There is a small sward of greenery between the back of the cottage and the graveyard below the old church. Willows trail their locks like fronds on the long grass surrounding the pond there, and they dip in the water like a nymph's hair. I watch the moon's gleam shine on and then sink into green water made darker by night. There is something transportative in such a sight, something mildly but disconcertingly uncanny. Willow trees are always feminine, I feel. And ponds by moonlight are goddesses. The clock on the church's steeple, high above the graveyard, is pale and badly lighted, and sometimes it resembles a pale watchful face. Behind me the cottage door is open, and the yellow glow of the light from the kitchen shines after me, as if in pursuit, but does not touch me. It is as though I have strayed to the edge of the safe shallows, to where the waters are uncertain and depthless.

I have not passed beyond the gate. Not yet. I have not had the strength, physically or mentally, to do so. But I will. In time. I am determined in that.

We buried Francesca on a Thursday morning, just before noon. The ground was hard, the sides of the grave raw, an exposed wound. My family was there. But I was all the family Francesca had since the death of her grandmother, the woman who'd raised her, and so it was a quiet gathering. Some kin I'd proved to be, I reflected; I who having found her had let her go without a fight, I who had failed to protect her when the wolf came.

The wind blew, turning the crowns of the yew trees and the willows so that their leafless limbs danced and coiled in lifeless tresses. It didn't rain. Frost transformed the grass into white coils of snakes and the paths were slick with damp. The Anglican vicar spoke some words that had no meaning to me, and after he had finished, when I heard the first pattering of soil fall onto the closed coffin, I almost went insane. I thought of her trapped there, confined in her wooden box with its silk lining. I thought of her eyes snapping open in the darkness, of her tearing her fingernails against the lid, desperate to be free, crying out so we might hear her and unearth her, and in doing pull her out in time to save her.

Try as I might, I could not stem the images. They came quickly, one on top of the other. I thought of how she must look in her grave, after all he'd done to her. He'd disposed of her in the river. She had been found relatively quickly, but the waters had still had their way with her. How pale her skin was on the mortician's table as I identified her, how raw the flapping cut at her throat was, how knotted and twisted her soft hair after the day in the water. He had placed his marker inside her mouth and bound her lips with tape. His marker was a moth. It had some meaning to him, though he wouldn't speak of it. Sometimes I thought of it buzzing there, alive still as Francesca lay dead. Fluttering in the dark, beating its wings against the cavity of her mouth, at the cold lifeless lips.

I thought of every moment she did not exist: how she did not wake in the morning to demand more sleep, how she did not get up and fail to make the bed because beds weren't for being made but slept in; how she did not brush her hair and munch on cereal until she was ready to face the world. Every moment of the world's turning I thought of her, and how she did not experience it, and I went crazy at her loss, found myself demanding the planet reverse its spin until it stopped at where she fell and allowed me to pick her up and rescue her.

He had taken her from me, and yet I could take no revenge on him. Already he lay awaiting his own grave, having taken his life in the prison cells. The police found a book he kept, in which there were cuttings of hair taken from the other girls he had presumably sent to early deaths, beside illustrations of moths. It was bad luck undid him. Had he taken another route to the river in his old dark car he might not have been seen throwing Francesca's body in the water. But once spotted his car was swiftly traced, and the police dropped on him soon after. I found I had no feelings for him. Isn't that strange? This man had taken so much from my world, and yet I couldn't find it within me to hate him. He displayed no remorse when he admitted his crimes, as if, the police detective told me, his acts were no different from those of a child removing the legs of an insect. I found I could not hate such a man because I did not see him as a real human being, rather a hole in the shape of one.

He had seen his opportunity at the German fair and taken it. I would never know at what point he intercepted Francesca. Whether it was at knifepoint or just by steering her from me as the crowds thickened around him and between us, like the deepening snow a wolf prowls through. No doubt as I was left standing waiting for her she was in his car already, already heading out of the city terrified and praying for me. After that . . . How I wish it would become unthinkable. But it does not. After that it flashes in my head in a series of punches and slashes, in graphic images I cannot shake free. I scream at them.

The evening after the funeral I took the frog from its plastic bag once more, and placed it on the mantle beside Francesca's clock. Its small baseball bat was in its mouth, a paler timber than the cha-cha wood the frog itself was made of. I stared at it for some time and then sat on the sofa and watched flickering images moving silently on the television, until the night became unavoidable and I knew I must go to the empty bed. As I shut off the TV and video and checked the locks, just before heading upstairs I took the frog in my hand, rubbing my finger over its spine, the ridges I should run the slugger over to make the croaking effect. I don't know what I was thinking when I wrapped my fist around the wood and took the carving with me.

Taking a moment to recover my breath at the top of the stairs, I took the bat from the frog's mouth. The sounds of the house settling around me filled my ears like wads of cotton. I held the frog flat on my palm. I noticed a small hole the size of a pin prick in the swollen part of the bat, and thought it must be to add resonance to the sound when it stroked the frog's back.

Because there was nothing else to do and I had already lost everything, as a single tear rolled down my cheek, I lifted the frog out before me, ceremoniously, and played the baton over the frog's spine. The high pitched croak filled the landing as the heat from the downstairs fire faded. I played the sound again.

From the closed door to our bedroom, I heard a frog croak back.

Now, these months later, as summer is here and the nights grow shorter, the evenings longer, I walk to the gate that leads beyond the garden to the stream and the pond, and beyond that, the graveyard where my love lies buried. Each dusk, though my condition continues to worsen, I venture out to the gate. I stand beside it, getting my second wind as the heat of day dies and a cold but not unwelcome chill plays over my skin with the loss of the sun. I swing the gate open then, content to hear its groans, the ones that a little oil could cure. They have become companions to me now, a part of my ritual. I have not yet gone beyond the gate, but it is only a matter of time before I will, I am sure.

She has come to me so often now, since I first stroked the frog and made it speak. When I play the bat over the ridges on the frog's back, the call hangs in the air anticipating an answer. It always receives one.

I have not seen her face, have felt only her presence beside me in the bed, or else heard her footsteps climbing the stairs at night. A shadow that should not be there disengages from its fellows and moves with no apparent cause, and I know it is her. More and more, I am drawn out here, to the edge of the garden, to that point beyond the shallows of my home.

I have seen a glow, soft and green, as green a light as ever Gatsby was drawn to, and I know it is Francesca. But I have not the strength to go so far just yet, and in truth I do not feel that I have been invited to. So I do not leave the garden to see her. But one day soon I know I will hear the croaking beyond the stream, will follow its resonance into the night. Its throb on the air will lead me on, and I will stare down into the green froth covering the pond. And when invited, when I hear that special call, I know I will plunge in and join her, my suffering finally at an end, and we will be together again, my love and I. I will have found her once more, and I swear that we will never be parted.

punching the
dark

Joshua Wiley had three reasons for not getting in the taxi that night. The first was the most obvious; he had next to no money on him and doubted he could pay the fare if it was expected of him. The second was that he didn't know where they would be going and he had never liked mystery tours, much less journeys to unspecified destinations after midnight. He got a shiver at the idea of arriving in some slum and finding himself threatened with a baseball bat spiked with nails; he might have to hand over more than his sadly depleted wallet and what remained of his dignity. The third reason was perhaps the oddest. The girl.

"Honey."

That's what she'd told him her name was.

He couldn't remember asking. In fact, he couldn't remember much of anything once he'd got past the first hour of the evening. He just didn't care. It had all begun to blur into one long yawn and his thoughts were slowing to the point where he feared they may stop altogether and he'd have to be carted away to some asylum for them to apply the jump leads and juice him with electricity to get his brain going again. He'd vaguely been wondering where Diana had gotten to and how much longer he was expected to endure this evening and then the girl, Honey, had appeared.

Diana was, theoretically, his date. As far as Josh could see, though, their evening seemed to have amounted to nothing more than walking in the hotel together and being shown to various corporate people in the big room where the party was being held, before she'd unhooked herself from his arm and gone into a quiet corner to speak to an older attractive woman who fawned over her with more than casual affection. They clearly had a relationship of some sort going on. Josh had begun to think he was nothing more than a smoke screen. The pair had disappeared not long after that and Josh hadn't seen them since.

Resigned to an unspecified time of social torture before Diana returned to find him, he'd wandered around circulating, listening in on conversations, the topics of which he knew next to nothing about. He sipped at the champagne flute that had wound up, by some magic, in his hand. He smiled at jokes when it was appropriate, and put on a solemn face of consideration when a debatable point was raised. Before anyone asked him who he was and what he did, he drifted away to the fringe of another conversation. He wasn't comfortable here. All of these people made more money than him and seemed gilded with success. Josh felt about the size of an emaciated rodent in a room full of overweight felines. He was, to put it in a blunt statement, having an awful time and right now it didn't look like that was going to change before dawn.

After what seemed like an unendurable eternity (it might have been an hour, if he were to believe his $25 Sekonda wristwatch), the girl appeared as he was floating between groups and they got talking.

"You're called Honey? Really?" he said. "Well, I suppose it's appropriate."

He had to say that it suited her. If bees had wound together a woman from their hive then this girl before him would be the result. The honey colouring ran all the way through her. Even her eyes contained glints of amber speckled across a tantalising shade of hazel. He imagined that her heart buzzed rather than beat. She was wearing a black dress with subtle yellow highlights, a real knockout that did all the right things for her. Or maybe she did all the right things for *it*.

"I'm Josh. Joshua Wiley."

He offered her a smile and his hand.

She took both. He noticed she wasn't wearing a wedding ring. And yet she was about his age, in her early thirties, and didn't seem the sort of girl anyone would abandon to a shelf. She said, "Joshua, do you mind me saying you look to be having a terrible time?"

"Me?" The fake-happy look he'd been wearing barely faltered. "Nah, I love coming to places where people I don't know talk about a business I know nothing about and the girl who brought me here ditches me the second she's introduced me to the important people she wants to impress and then goes running off, possibly to canoodle with a really attractive lady of indiscernible years. It's the sort of thing I live for."

She smiled at that, dimpling her cheeks. She didn't have a drink in her hand. He thought about offering to seek one out for her but couldn't find the grace to do so. He was still grumpy. All her attractive didn't make up for that.

"So tell me, Joshua, what do you do when you're not hanging around parties you wish you weren't attending?"

Josh told her the truth, that he worked in HR for a hospital. "Human Resources is my passion in life," he deadpanned.

She shook her head. "You're too pretty to work in a job like that. You should be a model or something. One of those guys you see sitting on sailing boats somewhere where the sea is green, salt spray in your hair. You've got the chin and the eyes for it."

Coming from her – she could have been a catwalk star, no question – that was a real compliment. But Josh knew his limitations. "Wouldn't work," he said. "I photograph really badly. It's true – I seem to come out looking like I weigh forty pounds more than I do. Imagine a real life Fred Flintstone and that's me in pictures. I think it's because of my nose. You need a thin nose to look good in pictures. If the nose doesn't work then nothing does."

"You sound like you've made a study of it."

"I work in HR for a local hospital. So of course I've made a study of it. I've made a study of everything.

I've read everything from scientific journals to the flotsam you see printed about celebrities every week. I've read dictionaries from start to finish and enjoyed the plot each time. What else would I do with all that time sitting behind my desk?"

"You know something, Joshua. I like you. I thought I would. I may come back for you."

Josh raised his champagne flute, in an ironic toast to his night. "I'll probably still be here," he said, turning to glance around for Diana. When he brought his attention back to Honey, she wasn't there. Maybe he'd imagined her. It was turning into that kind of an evening. He lifted the flute to his lips, drained it, and went in search of a refill.

Diana didn't reappear. He began to wonder if she really had sneaked off with the older lady with whom she'd been flirting. He'd been half joking when he'd told Honey that his date had hooked up with a woman. Now it seemed like a real possibility. Increasingly bored, Josh sauntered around from group to group, counting his footsteps, until he couldn't keep up the pretence of vague interest in subjects he could care less about.

Josh peeled away from the party and took a time-out on a leather-effect sofa in the foyer for a while, hidden behind a pair of spidery shrubs of some kind, until he needed to go in search of the bathroom. When he came back a couple were groping each other on the sofa so he turned around and reluctantly walked back toward the party.

"Oh come on," he muttered when he saw it was after midnight and Diana still hadn't returned.

The rest of the hotel was open for business. It wasn't just the conference room. It seemed to be a 24-hour sort of place. He thought about going door-to-door through the upper storeys to find her. It was an absurd idea, though. Who would do a thing like that? But what else was left for him to do? He didn't have her phone number so he couldn't ring her and tell her he wanted to leave. They lived in the same apartment block and that was how they knew each other. Back in the days when he had a cat (an inheritance from his deceased sister), she'd fed her while Josh had gone on holiday. This was also when he had a fiancé and his heart wasn't a crooked mesh of damaged goods. But, you know, time passes, things occur. Two days ago Diana had arrived at his door, an apologetic look on her face, and asked a favour. "It won't cost you a penny. I'll pay for everything. And it'll only take up an evening. Pretty please . . ." She was attractive in a Barbara Streisand way and had good legs. It shouldn't be a chore, he had thought, and who knows, maybe they could end up naked at the end of it all.

Hence him being here, and now wishing he wasn't.

With the time closing in on one o'clock, the party started to wind down. Diana still hadn't come back from wherever she had disappeared to.

Josh decided to hell with it, he was done waiting. A favour was a favour and a date was a date, but being taken advantage of – and this certainly felt like being taken advantage of – was beyond a joke. He'd save his best sour look for Diana when he saw her next and make it clear any apology she might offer would only be accepted grudgingly. But right now, he was leaving.

"Have a good time, sir?" someone asked him as he headed through the foyer and to the twin doors that led outside.

He didn't see the speaker, didn't care, and just raised a hand, replying, "Like you wouldn't believe."

Out of the fug of the hotel he took a lungful of the night air. It was colder than he had expected. To cap his night, snow was falling. It was the kind of snow that hangs in the air, seeming to float like constellations. It hadn't been forecast and he didn't have the jacket for it. Didn't have the shoes for it either. These weren't walking shoes. They were barely even standing around in shoes. One of the things he promised himself was that when he had the money he was going to buy the best damn shoes he could afford. He'd thought he was going home with Diana, sharing a ride. Now look at what had happened. He was going to wind up ruining his shiniest footwear walking slushy sidewalks because he couldn't spare the money for a cab, and after a mile his feet were going to feel like someone had hammered a hundred nails into each of them.

Sighing, he stepped down onto the sidewalk, hunching his shoulders and turning his collar up, resigned to an even worse end to the night than he'd previously divined. That's when he saw her again.

"Hey Joshua."

"Hey Honey."

She smiled and did a little wiggle, went "Boop-boop, de-boo," as if she'd had a drink or three too many and wanted the happy time to continue.

But he wasn't in the mood. Joshua Wiley was a nice guy but he had limits and he had been pushed to them. He wasn't in the right place for cutesy stuff. He ran a hand through his hair, looking around as he sought out words. There was exasperation in his voice as he said, "So what's your last name, Honey? You never said. Or are you like a hooker? I don't have any money if that's what you're hoping for."

"Well, thank you, Mr Grumpy. Sounds like you had a really good night."

She was standing with a purse held across her lap. Flakes of snow landed in her hair. The flakes had landed on her eyelashes, too. When she blinked little avalanches were set off. She was doing her best not to shiver, but even from here Josh could see the gooseflesh on her skin.

"A good night? Don't ask," Josh told her. He was about to set off for home. He'd have to use the A. He might have enough cash for that. If not he could pull some out of an ATM. Whatever, he wasn't going to compound the nightmare of the evening by spending a fortune on a taxi. He doubted Diana would reimburse him his fare. Before he went, he knew he owed Honey an apology. He held up a hand to her and shook his head. "My bad, and really, I'm sorry I snapped at you. Have a good night, Honey."

"Wait," Honey said. "Please."

The please made him stop. There was something real in it. He turned around.

She shrugged, looking too embarrassed to say what she needed to.

"Aren't you cold?" he said.

She wasn't wearing anything on top of the dress. Apart from the straps of her black and yellow number, her shoulders and arms were bare. She had on dark hose and pumps. Was she really a hooker? He'd thrown the line out without thinking. Now Josh wondered if he'd missed the fact that she was a sex worker earlier. It was possible. He wasn't used to being propositioned by call girls. Joshua Wiley wasn't that kind of guy. He didn't move in the circles that call girls frequented. He went to author readings at Barnes and Noble and read the newspaper on his Android tablet in Starbucks. He watched sports at his local bar and his social life consisted of hovering over the *Confirm Sign-up* button on dating apps. Now here was this beautiful woman, standing shivering before him and he'd called her a prostitute. Maybe he'd read this all wrong.

When she didn't answer him, he said, "Hey, come on. It's snowing. You *must* be cold."

"A little bit."

"What are you doing out here like that, then?"

"Waiting on a taxi. Want to come with me?"

The surprise wasn't that he didn't say no straight away; the surprise was that he asked her, "And go where?"

He half expected her to say *your place or mine* but

she didn't. She put a finger to her lips, looking apologetic. "Can't say. It's a secret."

"Then no, no thank you. I'm not in the mood for secrets. I think I had one pulled on me already tonight and I don't need another." By now Josh was certain Diana was shacked up with the woman somewhere in the hotel, in one of the rooms rising above him in the speckled night air. Sure, Diana had gotten naked tonight, but not with the person Josh had hoped.

Honey crossed to him, moving through the swirling snow, just as a cab pulled in. She hooked her fingers around his arm. "Some secrets are worth learning, Joshua. Don't you think?"

Josh should have known better. He *did* know better. You don't get to adulthood without learning some basics of survival, however square and vanilla a life you've lived. Getting into a cab with a strange girl with only a single name was a big no-no to someone like him. But for some reason, he felt reckless enough to go along with the stuff he should have been running away from. Maybe it was the cold, maybe it was the ache in his heels, the thought of a long walk whichever way he decided to go home.

"Come on, Joshua."

She pulled the rear door open. The cab's engine was running, the exhaust gathering on the air. The windows had dark films on them, the sort that made it hard to see through from the outside, but from the inside they would be quite clear. Josh stood there, hands rooted in his pockets. He ran through his reasons for not wanting to get in there, his lack of money, his natural dislike of mystery tours, and the oddness of the girl. But it was cold out here in the night. And what kind of trouble could a slip of a girl like this get him into? Really? He wasn't a tough guy, but he was no pushover. He did some gym work and had done half a self-defence course. Sure, if she pulled a gun or took him somewhere where a bunch of bozos could beat up on him then he would be in trouble. But for some reason he couldn't explain, Josh didn't think any of those scenarios would play out if he went with her.

He didn't know exactly what would happen, but he knew it would be something different.

On that last score he was dead right.

Honey was just leaning back from having spoken to the driver when Josh dropped onto the seat beside her. He clunked the door shut, registering somewhere at the back of his mind that it seemed inordinately heavy, a sign that he was tired and the late hour was getting to him. He missed whatever address Honey had given the guy behind the wheel.

Josh pushed himself back, wriggling a little to get comfortable. The seat was frayed, with its innards spilling out where the plastic had been torn. Josh sighed, finally placing his behind where it wasn't going to be too uncomfortable. The rear compartment of the cab was dark. It smelled, but Josh couldn't place the scent. It wasn't coming from Honey. She wasn't wearing any fragrance that he could detect. When he thought back to the party in the conference room, he didn't recall her being doused in some high-end cologne then either. Almost all the other women he had been close to that evening had been walking chemical clouds. Diana had dosed herself up, and so had the female bosses she'd introduced him to. But not Honey. She had been an absence of olfactory pleasures. And as far as Josh could tell, she still was. Whatever he could smell in here, it must have been left by the last passengers. Josh rubbed his thumb over his fingers, pulling a face as he realised they were greasy from handling the door handle.

Honey brushed up against him, her leg sliding alongside his own. He felt a charge of eroticism move through him and tried not to shuffle in his seat.

"I'm so pleased you came, Joshua. You won't regret it. I promise."

The heater must be on high, because he was getting hot. A trickle of sweat slid down the back of his collar. He wanted to wipe his forehead but didn't want Honey to think she was responsible for raising his temperature. When he'd caught his breath, he managed to say, "It's nice to be out of the snow."

"Isn't it? Though I kind of like it. It changes the world, makes you see everything differently."

"I hadn't thought f it like that."

Josh should have been watching the roads, to see where they were going, but Honey had a way about her. Something witchy. She demanded your attention, as if your eyes couldn't look away from her. Plus, right now, for all his discomfort, he wanted to look at her. He was getting turned on just sitting beside her.

"You looked so brave in there," Honey said. "That woman you came with, she's a fool. She shouldn't have abandoned you like that. I'd never have let you out of my sight. Anyone could come along and snatch you up."

"Maybe they have," Josh said. He managed not to groan but it was a close thing – he'd never delivered a line like that in his life and it sounded so corny now.

Honey laughed pleasantly. Her teeth showed when she smiled. Perfect white teeth in warm lips that hadn't been rouged artificially and were a sort of warm brown, reinforcing his notion that she was in some way a manufactured creature, something made by the hive. She came in and out of focus as the interior illumination of the cab waxed and waned, an effect of the cab speeding between streetlights. She was beautiful and Josh's doubts returned to him now. That rational part of his mind, the one that had flagged up three immediate reasons not to get in the cab, made itself heard again. Coming back to and staying on the third item on his list: the girl. Just what the hell was he thinking? She couldn't want anything he could give her, surely. This couldn't end well.

"You know, I'm having second thoughts about this. Maybe I can get dropped off home. I'll pay for my bit of the trip," he said, hoping he had enough in his wallet to cover the distance they'd come so far. If not he'd give the driver his watch.

He leaned forward to rap on the glass and speak to the cabbie through the vent slits. But Honey reached across him and, surprisingly strong, pushed him back into his seat. "Oh, don't do that, Joshua."

He didn't fight; he didn't know the procedure for fending off girls in the back of cabs. So he just sat there. She said,

"Stay. You don't even know what we're doing, silly. When we get there you'll kick yourself for even thinking of bailing out."

He tried not to fidget. "I don't usually do this sort of thing."

"Oh, I can promise you that you'll have *never* done this sort of thing. Honestly. Very few people have."

"Why am I suddenly not liking that fact?"

She said, not unkindly, "Because you're a big cowardly wuss, Joshua Wiley. That's why you work in Human Resources. Now shut up and enjoy yourself. Let your inhibitions go for a change. I'm not going to hurt you. And you might actually like whatever it is we end up doing tonight."

" 'Whatever it is we end up doing' ? You mean you don't know?"

Her eyes went sort of dreamy, she was travelling in her memories. "It's different every time. You don't know what you're going to get. But it's wonderful, Joshua. It's really wonderful. Usually."

Josh shook his head, unable to believe what was happening to him. He looked out the window. Snow sped by, buildings, other cars, then quiet streets, dull lamps. Tall narrow houses with closed doors. This was crazy. "Where are we? I don't recognise this."

He had thought he was pretty conversant with the city, that even if he didn't know every street he at least had a clue as to all the boroughs. The buildings they passed were high brownstones, neglected, the windows dull. Only a few were lighted and he had a sense that there was something wrong with those lights, a sort of stained dirtiness. Empty lots began to appear between the buildings, they looked bombed out and overgrown. It was disquieting. He saw no one on the sidewalks. The parked cars they passed sat on sagging tyres and looked as if they hadn't been moved in a hundred years. "What part of the city is this?"

"Relax yourself, Mr Pooh. We're nearly there."

"This doesn't look like the kind of neighbourhood where I could relax."

He thought about Diana, how none of this would have happened if she'd been straight with him and told him what to expect of their evening together. When she'd knocked on his door and asked for a small favour she'd been dressed up, wearing dark tights and showing some cleavage. There had definitely been suggestions that weren't openly stated in her invitation. She'd been playing him, he supposed. He glanced at Honey, saw she was smiling still, a kind of dreamy drugged smile. Maybe he was being played again. It was turning out to be quite the night for it.

"Really," he said. "This isn't the kind of place I could relax. I'm serious."

"That's why not many people get to see this, Joshua."

"I'm not going to get mugged, am I? Because I tell you now, I don't have much worth mugging. Look at this, see how much is in there. I don't even know that I can afford this fare."

"Put that away. And don't worry about the cab, it's paid for. No one's after your money, Joshua."

He fumbled for a joke. "Well, I warn you, my body's sacred."

They left the brownstones and the spaced out loneliness of the empty lots behind them, and entered a tunnel made of old red bricks with mortar so thick it looked like furred arteries. Even from inside the taxi, the sheer rankness of the tunnel was impossible to miss. It swamped whatever scent had troubled Josh before. At some time in its life the tunnel must have flooded and had never quite been cleaned out afterwards. Added to that, there were no overhead lights; the deeper they went, the less Josh could make out. Darkness felt to be pushing up against the sides of the cab, wanting to get in. Only the headlamps told Josh they were still in the tunnel – well, that and the echo of their passage as the vehicle continued on – otherwise he might have imagined a boundless country night weighted with clouds curled over the cab.

"You know what I dislike about Human Resources?" he said. When Honey didn't comment, he carried on, talking to ease his nerves. "That what I do is utterly meaningless. You know I had to take an exam for the role? An exam in pointlessness, to be sure I could perform pointless duties. I sit in front of a computer all day shuffling names on a screen. Every day, that's what I do. And I wasn't joking – I did start reading a dictionary to kill the boredom one time. My office doesn't have a window. When it's winter, I don't see daylight except for on my lunch hour. Which is more like forty minutes because of how long it takes to get out of the building and through all the security checks and back in again. Forty minutes of daylight for nearly five months of the year. I'm not even well paid. Everyone back in that conference room, at the party? Every single person there makes more money than me. Probably even the wait staff, too."

He looked at her. She was perfect, acclimatised to the interior, as if the snow had never touched her and the darkness was in awe of her. It had only taken a few minutes for the snow to soak into Josh's jacket. He felt like a dog that had come in out of the rain. He bet his hair was a mess. He had good, thick hair with a pronounced widow's peak. It needed maintaining, had a tendency to curl behind his ears and around his neck. Gel. Grooming. That was what it needed. The rain would have made it a mess, he knew that without looking to see it was so. But Honey looked like the bad weather had only come visiting, apologised for intruding, and then had left without leaving a mark on her. The bad smells didn't seem to trouble her either - the pre-existing scent in the cab and the mouldy damp from outside. It was all Josh could do not to wrinkle his nose. He settled for massaging his forehead.

"I bet you do, too," he said when he was done. "I bet you make more money than me."

She laughed, a delightful peal of happy bells chiming. She sounded high. "What is wrong with you, Joshua? Will you shut up?" She wasn't scolding him.

He sat back, hands across his lap, facing forwards,

his face set and unmoving, watching. The beams of light from the cab coning the way ahead, the tunnel going on, the silhouette of the man behind the wheel. "I don't do this kind of thing," Josh said quietly.

Honey put her hand on his thigh and Josh jerked involuntarily. Such a *sensation* ran through him. Static electricity. *Something.* But she didn't look as if she had noticed, or that she cared if she had.

"It's okay. We're nearly there."

A moment later they sort of bulldozed into a glue of darkness; a foul blackness seemed to wrap around the cab, congealing over its frame. Just as Josh was about to cry out in alarm they burst through it, and wherever they were it was suddenly daylight.

No, not daylight. That was impossible. It was . . . something else. Wasn't it?

"What are those? Spotlights?"

Josh was squinting. He lifted a hand across his eyes, angling it to block the dazzle. The inside of the cab lost its shadows. The light, well, it was pristine, so bright he couldn't think of anything to compare it to. Even lightning was shabby by contrast. This was a light of utter pureness. Put it to a prism and it would not split and reveal its component parts, of that Josh was utterly certain. It fanned in through cracks in the body work of the cab, bled around rivets and shone in wide sails from the edges of the doors.

Now he had some understanding as to why the windows had been darkened in the cab. They reduced the glare. So what, he had thought, upon seeing the film as he'd got in? Cabs and their drivers were endlessly quirky. He'd been in cabs decorated with cruciforms and hanging Jesuses, and in other cabs that looked like the driver's kids had finger-painted the interior to look like some crazy world of the Jurassic period. At one time he'd sat in a cab that had been tiled to look like a mosque. Darkened side windows were hardly worthy of comment. Until now.

"Is this why the windows are dark on the outside? To protect us from this light?"

"Here, put these on. They'll help."

These were sunglasses. And not just any sunglasses, Josh saw. Top of the range Raybans. Very expensive. He'd seen them behind counters in department stores but never dared to try any on. When he slid the arms over his ears and opened his eyes, he found that he could see perfectly well. It was like being out on a nice day. The kind our eyes have evolved to enjoy. But he couldn't make out any specific details of the world beyond the cab.

"Honey, what the hell is going on here?"

"We've arrived." She patted on the glass divide. She was wearing raybans herself. "Thanks, Ernie."

The driver lifted a hand. "You're welcome, Honey. Have yourself a good time. Don't let anythin' bite."

This was some sort of shared joke. They both laughed. Josh didn't get it and Josh didn't like it.

"I think I should go home," he said.

"Oh, shut up and get out." Honey opened her door, allowing the light to swell into the cab as one amorphous mass. Josh swore he felt it touch him and tried to scamper away from it, but there wasn't enough room and nowhere to escape to. It wasn't stupidly hot, as you'd expect such a light to be. It wasn't cool either. It was just right, like the prefect body temperature or lying in a nicely relaxing bath. Honey swivelled out of the cab and stepped away. A second later Josh's door opened and she was there, her hand out to him.

"I promised you a secret and this is a good one."

Josh hesitated. Ernie leaned all the way around. He was wearing shades, too. And a Yankees cap. He was pale faced, but carrying a lot of stubble. Josh couldn't see his eyes. The lenses were too dark. When he spoke, his teeth were every bit as perfect as Honey's. Josh really hadn't expected that. "Go on, guy. Get out there. I'm leaving soon, and you ain't coming with me, that I promise you. A trip like this costs, and you ain't got the money, you already said so yourself."

For a moment Josh thought about arguing. He could always stop at an ATM, he nearly said. But part of him didn't want to hear that the kind of currency you needed to pay for a trip like this couldn't be taken out of a cash machine.

Without saying another word, he edged out of the cab. His shoe touched something solid, though Josh didn't think it was asphalt or a stone sidewalk. It felt clean and without blemishes, like perspex or a vinyl floor. It didn't give under him and held his weight without complaint. Honey had her fingers around his hand. He'd barely realised. Now he clung to her as if afraid he'd fall through a cloud if he let go. Everything around them was so white and Josh was on edge. She seemed to think this was amusing. "I'm so glad you came," she said.

As Ernie's cab pulled away, driving into the light as if it were a fog, and swiftly becoming invisible, Josh looked around, trying to push his vision further ahead. All he saw was light, forms moving in it, never quite full, never entirely solid. Shadows on shadows, but inverted, so that they were whiteness on white.

"Honey?"

"Shh. Just enjoy it."

"I don't even know what *it* is to enjoy it. Tell me what I'm supposed to be enjoying?"

"I don't know how to describe it. I think it's bliss. That's the best I've ever managed."

Joshua wasn't sure he agreed. But equally he wasn't sure that he disagreed either.

He put his free hand out, spreading his fingers. There was nothing of form here, nothing of certainty, nothing to touch. He was an island in a sea of light, but he understood he could easily be swamped by it. He had the disconcerting feeling that were he to let go of Honey and slip beyond her, that he too might dissolve and become scattered on the vastness of the nothing, the perfect never-ending light that didn't cast a shadow. He and Honey were standing in the shallows of something vast, something possibly without a true end.

"Come with me?" Honey said.

"Where?"

"Into the light. All the way there. We're on the edge

here. It's better if we go deeper."

"What's deeper?" He wasn't sure he wanted to know.

Honey frowned. This was the first time he'd seen her pull any kind of puzzlement and uncertainty onto her expression since they'd been here. "I can't really remember. But I've been there before and I know it must be good. It has to be, right? Or I wouldn't want to do it again, would I?"

She tightened her grip on his fingers, and Joshua felt horribly as though she were waiting for assurance from him.

With nowhere else to go – he certainly wouldn't find his way out of here; there wasn't even a road for the cab to drive along now, as far as he could tell – going deeper into the light seemed like their only option.

"Well," he said. "I told you I didn't have anything worth stealing . . ."

A little later, he learned he was wrong about that. So, so wrong.

harry and
blight

"Are all English spies called Harry?" Blight wanted to know.

His posture awkward and stiff, Harry Morgan thought for a moment before answering. Not because it was a question he hadn't at some point asked himself before now, not after tripping over the name countless times in the work of Graham Greene and John le Carré, but because he knew that forked tongues shaped all conversations in the spy game.

As he looked out from the high vantage point of St Stephen's churchyard. to the flat fields and crooked ditches of the Romney Marsh, he thought wryly that some tongues forked more than others, his own included.

"You do get the odd *George* now and again," he said eventually, placing the stress in the sentence so that it couldn't be misunderstood. By doing so he'd elected to follow the course his superiors had suggested he might take should the opportunity arise.

George. George Hobson. Damnable thing, whatever it was happened to him. Know it was a while back. But find out if you can, why don't you, Harry.

Not quite shaped as an order. And thus meaning it needn't interfere with his duty. But still containing more than enough *Have a go all the same, old chap* for him to be able to ignore completely.

George. Do his bit by George – and in the process assuage any guilt remaining in the Service.

With his bait cast, Harry did his best to appear at ease on the uncomfortable slats of the bench he and his companion shared.

The light was crisp today, but toned in a softening gold he'd only ever found to be present at this time of the year. It burnished the reddening hedgerows weaving along the lanes across the marsh, tinted sheens of water amid the horizontal fields, though it made little impression on the breakers of the Channel beyond the long curve of the distant bay. The Channel, Harry thought almost nostalgically, across which so many invaders had swarmed, and more often than not been rebuffed and sent back, bloodied tail between their legs.

As he waited for Blight to speak, Harry caught sight of a couple of grey squirrels springing between gravestones toward the tangled autumn cover of the trees. The Norman church and its square tower looming a short distance behind his back shed an air of cold despite the sun.

Blight's features quickened with a smile. "Ah, yes. George. I remember George. Different league from you, though, wasn't he, Harry? Different time?"

"I saw him briefly, on and off, for a couple of years. He was moved up. A different section of the department from mine."

"Just starting out back then, were you, Harry?"

"Beginning to learn."

Harry thought it odd they were even having this conversation. Blight must know he hadn't been summoned for some debriefing or exchange of tactics. It wasn't as if this was the Cold War, a time Harry could almost look back on with happiness: men in creeping limousines playing Spy like they might a game of skill, calling truces to sip gin in a club and meet in deserted car parks at night . . . or in the grounds of a 12th century church overlooking the marsh. Well, there were echoes, that was undeniable, but Harry's rendezvous with Blight had nothing to do with such out-of-fashion enmities; they were games compared to the real wars being fought. Just games.

All the same, some of the traditions of those engagements remained.

"And you still don't know what might have befallen him? Your George, Harry? Doesn't that worry you?"

"We've taken precautions. Against eventualities we couldn't have foreseen back then. You'll find we're better prepared now." Harry hoped it was true.

"But you still don't know what happened to him."

"We still don't know the exact details of his . . . going," Harry admitted. He turned to face his companion. Blight was holding the tea Harry had poured from the steel flask, but he'd not drunk any of it. Not yet. Heat rose from the plastic cups, Blight's and Harry's own, in soft curls of steam. The sound of laughter from a wedding taking place in the nearby grounds of Lympne Castle, another old fortification standing on the rim of the marsh, drifted into the churchyard. They'd talked about dropping a notice on them, stopping the wedding for this operation. But now Harry was glad they hadn't. It was possible to hear so much in the laugher, he thought, happiness and a future unaware that the blink of a neglectful god's eye could lead to desolation. It was all too easy to make you melancholy if you thought about it for very long, the death, the destruction. Far better not to. Far, far better to hope for what might be.

He focused on Blight, while tightening his gloved hand around his own drink. He wanted him to understand he was serious when he made the offer. "You know any information you have would be listened to sympathetically."

"But would hardly alter the day's events, I suspect." Blight smiled once more, an act that caused Harry to pause.

He knows why he's here, Harry thought. *And he doesn't care.* Or if he did, then he wasn't showing it. *Maybe he's tired. God knows, we're all tired on this side of the Divide. Maybe he wants an end to it. Perhaps that's why he agreed to come. And not out of simple curiosity.*

As far as Harry was aware, no one had given consideration to that possibility. A chill stroked his spine. What else hadn't they prepared for? Suddenly this mission seemed a thousand times more dangerous than he had previously feared.

"Do you have a favourite season, Harry? Autumn was always mine." Blight sighed with an actor's air, perhaps aware that the man beside him was threaded with a listening wire. The monitoring team, who were sitting with headphones hard against their ears, in the discreet van in the lane behind the castle, had been hanging on Blight's words long before George's name was mentioned. Harry suspected that Blight was playing to them.

Blight said now, "There's something calming about it, don't you find? It's the evening of the year, when we think back on the day and look to the sky for signs of what tomorrow will bring." His dark eyes, dancing with the imps of devilry, met Harry's. "Given any thoughts to your own tomorrow, Harry? Tell me, are you much of a diviner?"

There was no way he was answering that; Harry knew the dangers of getting drawn into a personal conversation. "When George—"

But Blight wasn't listening.

"Do you know, I think you and Sandra should take those adorable little grandchildren of yours to the woods on the Downs. Let them enjoy the trees. It's the perfect time for it. Hannah especially will love the colours and shades."

If Blight was gauging Harry for a reaction, something hot and uncontrolled, then Harry did his best to disappoint him. Blight continued, barely containing his sly smile.

"Boys are different, though. I'd imagine Will would want to run riot, play outlaw or hunt for wild boar. I can't remember, have boar been reintroduced or is it somewhere else I'm thinking of?"

"Not here that I'm aware," Harry said all but formally.

"I'm sure Will would love to see one anyway. Hmm?"

Harry had been in the game long enough to know that Blight had pulled out his grandchildren's names in an attempt to unbalance him. Subtle leverage in conversation, that's what this was about: *I know things too, Harry.* Like the tease over what had happened to George.

It was all promises from ghosts, but no less alarming for that.

Standard practice was to move operatives' families into safe houses before commencing with this kind of action. Harry had driven his daughter's family to the Sussex bolthole himself, had twice looked over the security details. He'd walked the perimeter until he was satisfied all that could be done was being done. His grandchildren were safe behind the deep walls of the old rectory, a towering place of uneven roofs and new extensions, protected within three tiers of ash and hawthorn hedges. There were people there to see they came to no harm. Harry had to trust the Service to do its job.

All the same, he felt winded to hear this creature and its vile tongue shaping Hannah's and Will's names.

He did his best not to show it; his face, with its

beginnings of a hound dog droop, was impassive, his blue eyes cold. He hardened the defences around his thoughts. When he spoke, his voice was perfectly neutral.

"Very well, if you don't want to tell us anything about George, then I don't suppose you will," he said. But he knew he'd been quiet too long, a giveaway to someone like Blight. His opponent would know he'd thrust a rapier through Harry's armour. Trying to hide this, Harry raised his cup to his lips and drank, despite the tea being too warm for his taste and lacking his habitual milk. His darling Sandra made the best tea in the world, but of course she hadn't been allowed to prepare this flask. She'd be safe in Sussex, too, he reminded himself, whatever Blight might decide to say about her.

Blight chuckled, watching Harry go about recapturing his lost equilibrium.

"There's really nothing to tell about George, Harry. No point, not if you've prepared for everything. If you have, then you'll know what happened to your man. It would have been one of those eventualities, obviously. And if you know them all then it's just a matter of deciding which. It will give those clever bodies you employ, the ones who spend so diligently their days in front of computer terminals, something to do."

"You're sure you've nothing to tell me? It might go better for you if you have."

This time Blight's smile didn't even pretend to reach his eyes.

"Don't spoil this by dropping threats, Harry. That's

uncivilised."

Harry gave an all but imperceptible nod. Recovering George had been an unlikely result from the outset. In truth, the man was long dead – or damned. There was no bringing him back, and no matter what Harry's superiors might have hinted at, it was impossible that someone would sanction an exchange for him, even if he was by some unlikely chance in a tradable condition. They had the country to think about, after all, maybe more than the country; and if George returned there was always the chance of a passenger or worse hitching a ride with him across the Divide. The man could never be left unwatched.

But Harry felt he'd done right by his colleague in bringing his name up, while doing the very least as well.

"Or perhaps you've not been thinking about tomorrow at all, Harry," Blight said now, as if the last minute of their conversation hadn't taken place. "Perhaps you've been waiting to make sure you survive this first, before you let yourself think of other things. Family trips to the woods and so on. Now why would that be? And why you? They'd normally send someone with a few more years on them. Expendable sort of chap, that's the type they tend to use since George's unfortunate disappearance."

When Harry didn't answer quickly enough, Blight said, "Something inoperable is it? My sympathies if so. But they do say the knowledge of one's demise sharpens the senses. Makes one see things so much more clearly."

He turned from studying Harry's face, back to the view and its splendours.

Harry looked, too. St Mary in the Marsh was visible if you knew where to look, a few other small settlements in clusters of houses beside the lanes. Then there were the more noticeable landmarks: Dymchurch and its crowds of holiday caravans, the grey blocks of the power station toward the tip of the peninsula, out at Dungeness. When the sun was at the right height, Harry knew, it sometimes turned the sea golden around the bay further west. But not today, and not at this hour, appropriately enough.

"The trees are very red just now, aren't they, Harry? Do you notice that? I certainly do. I wonder if you see it as clearly as I?"

"Yes," Harry said, clearing his throat, "the trees are very good this year. But I always find that around here. It's the season."

"Defiance there, Harry? How's the saying go – the Welsh inebriate – rage against the night?"

"You'll find it's what we do. Drunk or sober."

Blight nodded. The scales on his hands were not so apparent in this light, but every now and again Harry saw their sheen under the hairless skin, most notably when Blight moved his fingers, an action both oddly mechanical and yet slippery with unnatural biology. Harry had been glad of his gloves when they'd met, hadn't wanted to touch Blight without some barrier between them. When this was over he'd destroy the thermos flask and the plastic cups, insist the bench was dismantled and likely burn the clothes he was wearing as well as the gloves. A long shower for himself afterwards, of course, as hot as he could bear, until he was breathing steam and his skin reddened and he wept.

"You're a despairing race, Harry. I don't pretend for a moment to understand you. You revel in your acts of brutality, yet at the same time you produce your works of art and eulogies for the deceased. Will there be a eulogy at your funeral, Harry? I find it hard to believe there'll be many words said about me when I'm gone."

"I'm surprised you care."

Blight thought on it for a moment. "I don't, I suppose. I shouldn't. Have I been in your realm so long to be thinking such thoughts? One should have thought one would have noticed."

Harry didn't say anything. He raised his cup, drank more of the tea. Blight followed suit. They sat in silence for a while, with the gentlest of breezes rattling the browning leaves of the trees that stood to the side of them. Harry kept his breathing steady, his expression steadfast and impassive, mental armour in place. Far away on the Channel a tanker seemed stationary, an immovable hulk of metal on the water.

"How long have you known?" Blight said at last.

"That you've become earthbound?"

Blight nodded, an admission. "Yes."

"We've had our suspicions for years now. Tracked you for quite a while. The London incident as good as confirmed it."

"Ah. Yes. London. But it's been happening since

before then, to be truthful. Well, everything was becoming so linear. I see Time as you see it now, Harry. I confess I find it discomforting to experience it as nothing more than motion, and all flowing in but a single direction. It affects one's thoughts so. For a while I tried to fight its currents, but one finds oneself carried further along the more one remains in the water. There are so many temptations in your world and it's hard to leave them voluntarily. You do rather bedevil us here, Harry, you really do."

"You can't stay, you know that. Not as you are."

"No. I suppose not."

"And if you can't return, if we can't tip you across the Divide . . ."

"No threats, please. And the Divide *is* a threat to me now, as much as it is you. But I do have some abilities remaining, Harry. Don't take everything for granted. There's always the possibility of the unforeseen, notions remaining beyond those you and your clever men with their electric thinking machines have planned for. Remember George and what happened to him, hmm? Mysteries, Harry. Mysteries."

Harry took a breath, glad to be upwind of Blight. There was much bluster and bluff in what Blight had to say. But it still stank. They both understood that Blight's abilities, as he called them, would continue to wane, that they would become harder to control and subsequently more dangerous. They'd interfere with physics for one thing. And that couldn't be allowed. Mothers in the shopping districts couldn't be permitted the surprise experience of levitation; choirs of trees sounding arias in the town parks were a non-starter; a downpour of slugs and snails would not grace the weather forecasters' reports. Metals would not bend and bleed for sight of the sun.

Harry's section of the taskforce understood how dangerous it would be to let Blight function without constraint, his powers becoming more and more slippery. If Harry gave the signal, the assassination squads were ready to slam into the churchyard and try their hand with traditional weapons; perhaps attempt to force a breach in the Divide and hurl Blight into it. But Harry didn't think that would be necessary; he hadn't from the start of the mission, to be honest, and certainly not now. Whatever else Blight might be he was talkative, and Harry had found through his vast reading on the subject that the talkative ones always gave an indication of when they'd turn dangerous.

So far Blight had only hinted, and then without much vigour. He seemed more the passive melancholic than the brimstone-scented reaper. Harry almost felt sorry for him. Besides, it was as good as over now. Meaning George would remain lost, another mystery, though of course the Service's files would report an attempt to retrieve him had been put into action and failed. Guilt assuaged in triplicate.

Harry lifted his cup to his lips and sipped at the tea, too sweet for his own taste, but in other ways just right. Blight stayed still beside him, his own drink, only half consumed, in his scaled hand.

"You still persist in calling us demons, Harry. Yet you know so much more about what we are now."

"We do," Harry agreed. "But it doesn't change how dangerous you are. Calling you by another name, hunting out a new classification, the effect's the same."

"Yet you cling to your medieval superstitions and what they have to say about us?"

"There's some worth in them."

"Really? I find it hard to express any."

"Comfort," Harry said. "Strength. Faith. Solutions to certain problems. Of need, say, and a form of worship, structure to a life. Continuation."

"Continuation? That damn linear thinking again. Starts and finishes."

"It offers defences, too," Harry went on. "Shield of love. Sword of truth."

"Hodgepodge trickery," Blight said dismissively. He sipped at his drink until it was done with, and now he leaned back. He held onto the cup though Harry didn't offer to replenish his share of the flask's contents. There wasn't the need. This time Blight cleared his throat before speaking. "There's . . . There's very little in your moderate God boxes that can affect the reality. Splinter of the true cross you're carrying for protection, is it, Harry? Spear from Christ's side to fling at me if I don't tell you about George? Or if I threaten to continue on, doing whatever I do on this side of the Divide. Indulging in my pleasures."

Harry said nothing.

"No, I didn't think so," Blight said. "Didn't think so at all."

Silence, a breathing thing. It continued for a while. Blight seemed to slump a little, as if tired.

"We don't need them, that kind of iconography," Harry said when it seemed certain Blight had nothing more to say. "Don't need to know about George either, unless it's something that's freely given, the only way we could trust you. The rest – the problem you cause by simply being here – I'm afraid it's solved already."

Blight hooded his eyes for a moment and then with a fresh inquisitiveness looked at Harry. Curious regard settled on the man, reading him ever so carefully.

Harry didn't resist, allowed part of his mind to be read, and saw no self-pity there when it was done, as realisation dawned in Blight. If Harry had wondered earlier about the creature being tired and ready to put an end to its time in this realm then his suspicions were confirmed now.

"I wouldn't want to go back," Blight said, apparently ready to accept what he'd found in Harry's thoughts. "Not after this. There's too much enjoyment here. This side of the Divide . . ." His lips twitched in cruel irony. "This side of the Divide is heaven. Enjoy it while you can, Harry, whatever your physician's diagnosis. Because what comes after is your unravelling. Time as eternity unbound. Unbearable even when you're insane. That's what it's like across the Divide. When the Divide finally collapses, it will unthread each strand of your world, and the weave of unknowingness will rip your universe to tatters."

Blight tried to say more, but his voice was fading, growing hoarse, and had become little more than a deathly croak toward the end.

Harry sighed, pushed up off his knees and stood. A small performance came of buttoning his coat. But he didn't need to hear any more. It was all as good as done, and he'd seen as much. Blight had found his body wasn't responding when he tried to move. He seemed sunken in on himself. Harry reached down and took the plastic mug from him, not looking beneath the hood and in Blight's face. He meant to extract it from Blight's grip gently, but even so one of the demon's fingers snapped off with it. Skin shed like a lizard's from around the bird-like bones.

Blight didn't appear to notice, or seem too bothered if he did. He was a shallow, reduced, piteous thing now.

"Superstition in the end," Harry said loudly enough that Blight might hear, though he knew the demon had already seen the truth of his poisoning when he'd looked in Harry's mind. All the same, Harry couldn't face him as he screwed the top onto the thermos flask. He turned away. The view across the marsh was a preferable sight anyway. So many invaders repelled from across that short stretch of water beyond, the English Channel. So many threats from so many quarters, the timid and grandiose to the near unimaginable.

"Water from the font, blessed in Jesus' name before it was brewed into tea, if you were interested," Harry said. "Your weakness is that you were becoming like us, forgetting what you are. You assume because I drink something it isn't harmful to you. But of course in this case it's quite deadly."

He was watching the occasional car glint along the winding tracks among the marsh fields, talking over his shoulder to the demon as he did so.

"Whatever happened to George, we'll find out one day. And when we're sure we can, we'll seal that way across the Divide. And any others."

Harry nodded as if to convince himself more than the demon. His eyes were set on far horizons.

"Comfort. Faith. Surety. We'll make our god big enough to do the job. One day."

He half expected a reply. Half expected Blight to point out how far in the considerable distance of the linear future that possibility lay, and that Harry and his grandchildren would long have been wishing insanity good riddance before then.

But when he turned to Blight he saw there was nothing left to have cared; even the demon's hooded gown was gone. Harry saw nothing but a disintegrating pile of dark flakes, a burned set of lizards' scales, falling through the slats of the bench, shifting to ash, until even that was gone, dismantled by the breeze. Leaving Harry standing there alone, lacking answers, but knowing he had done all he could do.

all that remains
of silence

It had been Jamie's suggestion that they leave the basket behind, but Emma wasn't having any of that.

"It comes," she said, and rolled him a warning look that said, *Don't mess me about on this one, Jamie. Not if you know what's good for you.* "If we don't bring it along, God knows what will happen. And you can be sure it'll do something to make us regret it – assuming no one else does beforehand. It always does."

Jamie tried to front up an argument anyway, the way a child will test the patience of its parents, knowing full well that there wasn't a chance it was going to have its way. "Maybe just this once, if we're not too late getting back from whatever the heck this stupid invitation's for . . ."

"It won't work. Again, assuming we *even get back* if we don't take it. You do know this can't be about anything else, don't you?" With some distaste she held up the invitation that wasn't simply an invitation, making sure there was the minimum contact between the envelope and her fingers, and waved it at him. "Right, Jamie?"

He heaved out a sigh. The thing was, he did know she was correct. He truly did. Leaving the basket unattended always brought on some kind of misfortune. But a self-destructive demon inside him *still* wanted to leave it behind, and never mind the "request" in the invitation.

"Jamie?" Emma said.

He shrugged, making the shoulders of his recently dry-cleaned suit pitch and yaw. "I guess you're right," he admitted. "But I'm sick of lugging this thing about with us everywhere we go."

She smoothed a hand over his lapel. Then she straightened the knot he'd put in his tie – he never could keep them square and in line. "One day, Jamie. One day we'll be free of it. I promise." Her lips were close to his, her eyes so large and shiny, like moonlight on secret wells of water.

"Damned thing," he said softly.

And it was.

"Come on," she told him, brisk and business-like once more. "The cab's waiting. If we don't hurry, we're going to be late."

"Then I'll fetch it along, I guess."

"I'll tell the driver we've got luggage."

The driver helped Jamie with the large basket and eased the trunk lid closed. "Boy," he said as the shocks groaned. "It didn't seem that heavy when we lifted it up. What have you got in there?"

"It tends to vary," Jamie told him as truthfully as he

could. He glanced at Emma, who sat in the back seat trying not to look concerned through the rear window. He figured she'd felt the weight of the basket change when it had gone in the trunk. She did her best to keep her face neutral. Her eyes couldn't hide her concern, though, not to someone who knew her.

"Well, I tell you, I've never seen the like." The driver lifted his cap and ran his fingers over his scalp. The wheel arches had sunk until they were almost touching the tyres. "You'd think we'd loaded up a wash tub judging by how she's riding. Not some square old wicker picnic basket. That's the oddest thing."

Jamie said nothing.

When the cab pulled up outside the Jefferson Building fifteen minutes later, Emma paid the driver. She handed over a fair but not extravagant tip. As she'd told Jamie many times, it paid to remain inconspicuous with your generosity in times of another person's great astonishment. A tip worth a couple of bucks wouldn't draw any more attention to them than the basket had already done, and it was likely that the cabby would have forgotten about the fare by the time his shift ended. But only, of course, if nothing else like a too generous tip caught his attention.

Now they'd arrived Jamie made sure to attend to the basket by himself while Emma distracted the driver. For a moment he feared the creepy load wasn't going to comply, because when he steeled himself and tugged on its handle, the damn thing didn't move an inch. Jamie swore lightly. The basket was still pressing on the cab's shocks, and Jamie feared that even with the cabbie's help he'd be unable to lift it free and drag it onto the sidewalk. There'd be no way that he and Emma could hope to be forgotten by him then.

"Are you all right, darling?" Emma asked as she turned around. She was careful to shield the cabbie's view of Jamie's actions, and pulled a face urging him to get on with it. She added, for show, in her sweetest voice, "We should probably get a move on."

"Sure," Jamie said, and through a quick surge of his expression the cabbie couldn't see, he told her this wasn't going so well.

Meaning for him to hurry up, no matter what the problem was, she said, "Eric and Lydia will be wondering what's become of us."

Eric and Lydia were fabrications, made up by Emma on the spur of the moment. No real names, Jamie remembered. Not in front of witnesses. Not their own or anyone they knew. It was always the way when they travelled. "Okay. Let me get the basket out," he said, and sent an unsentimental prayer to any minor deity that might bestow a favour. "Wouldn't want to keep Eric and Lydia waiting," he muttered.

This time when he pulled on it, the basket came up as if it was filled with nothing more than a litter of kittens.

"Thank you," he whispered and was still paying tribute beneath his breath when the cab drove away into the first tears of the rain.

Room 337 was on the fifth floor. Once upon a time, before the Jefferson Building had originally gone up, there'd been further floors scheduled to be built, and in some flight of whimsy, the architects had decided that it would be funny to put the highest number on the ground floor, so that Number One was all the way up in the clouds, the penthouse suite. But when the building project was scaled down and the architects were changed, no one remembered to reappoint the door numbers to their traditional sequence, so now, when you reached the top of the building they petered out in the mid hundreds, still counting backwards.

Emma told Jamie this as they turned the last corner of the stairwell. He took a moment to recover his breath, letting her pass by him into the hallway. After five flights, he needed a rest. Carrying the basket was by no means a breeze, but the danger of being trapped in an elevator with it and it altering its weight meant it paid to take the stairs. Emma stood at the ready, waiting for him, while he slumped against the wall signalling a time out. She was still telling him about the building.

"That's fascinating," he said when she'd finished.

"It pays to know your history." She took a handkerchief out of a sleeve and dabbed it over his forehead. "You're hot. You really shouldn't be so hot." She glanced at the basket, which he'd put beside his foot as he leaned above the tired wainscoting. He saw her consider touching it, perhaps trying to lift it and take some of the burden. But her hands bunched into fists even as she thought of the act. He understood, and it didn't matter if she were wearing gloves now or not, he recognised the revulsion she was experiencing. He grinned cruelly.

"Hard to do it, isn't it? Your mind's telling you there's not a problem, it's just a plain old wicker basket. It can't do you any harm. Why, that would be absurd. So just take hold of the handle and lift it up." A wing of hair fell from his forehead, covering one eye. He brushed it back into place and watched her, seeing how she was reacting. "Shouldn't be anything stopping you."

"But I can't do it," she whispered, held by some trick of mesmerism to *That Object*, as she sometimes thought of the basket.

"It's because your flesh knows," Jamie told her. "It knows what your carefully honed mind, full of learning and rationality, won't admit to. This thing here," he nudged it with his toe, showing great care and respect as he did so, "should not *be*. It shouldn't exist."

Emma couldn't find her voice. Some imp had stolen it and fled with its prize, exhibiting ghoulish glee at the crime.

Laughter cut along the corridor. It could have come from behind any one of the anonymous doors along its length. All the same, it sounded sourceless and did nothing to ease the couple's feelings. It was enough to break whatever deadlock they were stuck in. Emma dipped inside her purse for the envelope and with some discomfort opened it up, even though they both knew the number they were looking for. After reading the single sheet of paper again, she said, "Are you all right?"

Jamie nodded, pushing himself from the wall. "Sure."

"You're okay to go on?"

"Okay might not be the word. But yes. I can get us there."

There was no envy in her eyes as he leaned forward and wrapped his fingers around the basket's handle. He knew she'd be thinking of snakeskin, how it looked slick and oily but was anything but that when you put your hand against it. His face hardened as he made his grip firm. He stood up. Heavier. He was lifting a different weight than from earlier. "Never the same twice," he confirmed.

"Room 337, fifth floor," Emma said, and started to scan the numbers as she walked ahead of Jamie, putting a finger out to each door they passed.

It was as Emma was counting aloud that they were startled to hear something within the basket shift and drop with a heavy thud. Jamie staggered awkwardly, ready to deal with a change in weight. He spread his legs and fastened his knees, half-fearing he and the basket might go crashing through the floor.

"Jamie!"

"It's okay, its okay. It's no heavier," he said, revealing his surprise. He stood there, braced all the same.

"Then what—?"

"Shh! Hear anything?"

They listened. Jamie felt sweat slide down the back of his neck and sidle under his collar. He was aware of the noose of his tie, the heavy knot Emma had secured below his Adam's apple. With careful deliberation, he tilted the basket, experimented with its weight. He was holding it with both hands. But nothing slid or rolled or dropped or tipped over inside. In the most gentle manner he could manage, he bobbed the basket up and down, so that whatever had fallen loose inside would lift up and then drop down again. But nothing did.

"Still feels solid. But you know, I think it might be slightly lighter than a minute ago."

"My God, all this time," Emma said. "That's the first change I ever knew come over it while we're watching. Actually touching it."

"Yeah. Me, too."

"Maybe it's getting excited, knows where we're taking it. What do you think it means?"

"Why's it have to mean anything?"

"Because—"

"Uh uh. Because nothing. Nothing it's done has ever meant anything before." He'd come to believe that. Through all the nights he'd sweated sleeplessly, through every anxiety dream that had him contort beneath tangled sheets, he'd told himself the same thing over and over again: that there wasn't any meaning or intention behind the basket's existence. It just *was.*

"But this is different," Emma pleaded. "Isn't it? Before it's always been the same. We never see it happen. Only the results. How much it weighs when you pick it up again, which side it's lying on in the morning after we've slept. How it smells sometimes. The songs coming out of it. Can't you see that this is new? The fact that it's changed *while* we're in contact with it."

He couldn't. And he didn't like to be reminded of the songs, those old Glenn Miller tunes that seemed a staple of black and white war movies on cable channels every Sunday afternoon. He didn't know Emma had heard them, too. He recalled the night he'd woken to "Moonlight Serenade" and seen the basket glowing eerily in a corner of their darkened bedroom, casting angles out of true, and how there had been huge, comically contorted shadows that didn't have a distinct source moving around the bedroom walls. God, he'd been scared. He hadn't woken Emma, had just lifted the sheets higher and tried to shut out the noise, pretend the shadows didn't exist, and get back to his restless sleep. At some point the music had stopped, the light had winked off, and the shadows . . . Well, who knew? But he hadn't seen them again and prayed he never would.

With a nod to Emma now, he said, "Let's do whatever it is we came here for."

They found the door with the correct numbers on it, two threes and a seven. It was a pretty nondescript door, the kind you see in a hundred other apartment buildings. There was nothing fancy to distinguish it. No special handle or flourish around the blind fish-eye peephole. It was a door like any other, this one about thirty yards on from the stairs.

Jamie put the basket down. He stood to one side, while Emma stood to the other. They were like a pair of imitation cops flanking a suspect's hideout. Jamie looked at her.

"You wanna?" he said.

She didn't, but Emma reached out and rapped her knuckles to get the occupier's attention anyway, then quickly retracted her arm and stared into Jamie's eyes while they waited. When no one came and any voice failed to call out an hello, Jamie tried it. He made rapid percussion on the door, as if with a fist of dimes instead of his sharp knuckles. Feeling absurdly exposed, he wished he had a gun. A short-nosed revolver, of the sort a detective might carry in a Mickey Spillane thriller. His empty hands felt feeble without a weapon.

"What if there's no one here?" he wondered.

Emma didn't know. "Try again," she said.

He did, pounding with the heel of his fist this time, good strong knocks it would be impossible for anyone inside to miss. Both he and Emma heard the sound echoing through the apartment. But nothing seemed to change. He was going to say – and with something like relief – they should go back home, that this was a bust, some prank being played on them, when somewhere further along the hall a door unlatched and swung open. The voice of a young woman – a voice that, because of the tone and texture, Jamie took to be that of an African-American – sang out. "It ain't nothing, no bother of ours," before the door shut again.

Jamie shook his head, about to tell his wife they'd done all they could and it was time to retreat, they didn't want to attract any attention, when he realised something had changed. Emma saw the same thing that he did. While they'd been distracted by the noise down the corridor, someone had swung the door to 337 inwards a few inches. Not enough to reveal what was beyond by any means, but enough to suggest they'd been heard and here was an invitation to come in.

Any notion in Jamie's head that this was some prank was swiftly dispelled. They were expected. They'd been granted admission. Speaking in a communication of the eyes so loudly that Jamie thought his retina would split and deafen, Emma told him that she was with him, and that they should step inside. It was time.

"Okay," he whispered.

He went in first, using a toe to poke the door open gently wider on an open entrance hall. He brought along the basket. This time it was as heavy as an automobile battery.

"I don't see anyone," he murmured and stepped forward, giving Emma room to follow.

He looked around him. The wicker picnic basket he carried did not seem so very strange and out of place in the furnished corridor before them. If anything, Jamie felt it were he and his wife who were the alien beings embedded in a world in which they did not belong. Through his contact with the extraordinary basket – which Emma had only ever touched once, shying from its clammy feel not only in real life but even in her frequent and unwelcome dreams of it – Jamie had obtained a kind of immunity through exposure to the pervasive *otherness* that was also present in this small apartment. All the same, his every nerve rebelled at each new step he took, and he had to force himself to stutter onward.

"Hallway, with a few doors ahead," he somehow felt it necessary to record aloud.

"Oh my," Emma gasped, following after him.

"Take it easy," he said. "You get used to it."

He felt her hand seeking comfort at the small of his back, as if to anchor herself to a form of reality she understood. One in which strange wicker baskets did not change their weight at the whim of an unheared clock. One in which the architecture of a small apartment in a tired old housing block did not bow and stretch when you stared too determinedly at its straights and angles.

"Mary Mother of Christ," Emma began to whisper.

"Shh, shh."

Jamie made sure of his grip on the handle, determinedly trying not to consider his burden's weirder properties as they moved further on. But one thing had always nagged him, and it came back to him now. For the time he and Emma had been in possession of the basket, they'd never – not once – found a way into it. Though it showed well-oiled hinges and had a neat straw loop around a latch lock, these things were inviolably a part of a single connected whole, as a leg is to a mammal or a wing to a bird. The basket only looked like a basket. What it truly was, Jamie was scared of knowing. But he had a feeling he may be about to be shown. Because in the same way the basket felt like a living creature, so did the inside of 337.

"Stay close," he told Emma, and with his free hand he found her fingers.

They moved into the apartment, watchfully vigilant. They did not call out, nor announce their presence with a polite cough.

A woman of Asiatic appearance, in a deep blue blouse beneath a short serving apron, walked across the end of the hallway before disappearing into one of the doorways. She didn't glance across to look at them, and was gone so quickly she might have been a ghost. Something about her had trembled on the brink of existence, as if she were partly unreal; she'd seemed to crackle, as if she'd been super-imposed on film stock of the apartment. "Did you see that?" Jamie whispered.

"I did," Emma whispered back.

"Jesus."

"She didn't look real."

"What should we do?"

"I don't know."

They stood silently until Jamie said, "Tell me what the note says again."

"It'll be no different from before."

"Tell me anyway."

He didn't look around to see her fumble it, one-handed, out of her purse and slide the single sheet of paper from the embossed card envelope. "7-30, November 1. Room 337, Jefferson Building. Possession of object imperative. We will know. The presence of Mr and Mrs Jamie Purcell is required. Kind regards."

Jamie nodded, noted again the "required" (and not

the more usual "requested") that had so upset him earlier (along with the "We will know") when the note had been delivered. Well, slid under their door and brought to their attention by a series of three sharp raps. When Jamie had gone to catch the delivery boy, there was no one there.

"It's the same," Emma told him softly. "What were you hoping for?"

"Something different, I suppose. It seemed like a possibility."

"I think I understand."

A gong rang, and the uncanny maid – Jamie supposed that's what she must be – ratcheted out into the hallway like a mechanoid and passed through into another room. The door she went through closed behind her with the polite click of a latch dropping into place. But the doorway from which she'd come through into the hallway was completely silent, as if untouched. Again she was there and then she was gone, before more than the most rudimentary details about her could be gathered. Jamie realised he'd frozen at her appearance, and that the sounds she'd made, slippered feet pressing on the dull carpet, had seemed like the loudest thing in the world to him. Even louder than the thunder of his heartbeat.

"Do you think she knows we're here, Jamie?"

"I don't know. I'm not sure what she sees. If she does, she doesn't seem to care. Any thoughts?"

"We should go on."

"You're sure? We could turn around and leave."

"You know we can't do that."

He did. And regretted what must come next, because he didn't think it could be anything easy. He felt an unpleasant suggestion of a pulse coming from the basket handle, as if he were holding an excited creature, and remembered again that whatever the basket was, he knew for certain it wasn't a simple picnic basket. He shifted his attention to his surroundings, anything to distract himself from that thought. But it didn't much help. The walls this far in were composed of the same oddness of texture as the rest of the apartment. Though a casual observer would think that they were perfectly normal walls, with perfectly ordinary wallpaper pasted upon them, and from which were hanging the usual mass production prints and pictures, somehow Jamie knew that were he to reach out that he would come into contact with something alive and not altogether contained within the structures of standard space-time as he knew it.

"It's all the same," he told Emma, careful to float his voice on the softest of breaths. "The basket, this apartment. Even the maid. They belong together somehow. Don't keep your eye on anything for too long, or it begins to change. You can see it."

"While staying the same. Distorting. I understand."

She was doing well to keep her fear under control. Jamie was proud of her – and he was reminded of that great quality in her, one he'd not truly appreciated until after they were married: the ability to stand before a firing squad and feel immortal. He wished he'd half her strength right now. "I love you," he told her and felt her squeeze his palm in reply.

They passed an occasional table, stepped around a dark wood chair that seemed to bow as if its composition was more jello than varnished oak, and drew level with where the maid had machined in stuttering crackles of solidity across the hall. There was a single closed doorway that probably led to the kitchen (into which she'd last been seen heading), and opposite that, and to which they now turned their attention, was a wide double doorway. The panelled doors, painted an eggshell white, were pushed together. Jamie couldn't decide if they swung open or slid back on runners. The deeply recessed handles didn't offer any clues.

"What do you think," Emma said.

"It'd be where you'd expect someone to be, a dining room or something. But it doesn't look right."

"You feel it, too?"

"Something odd? Odder." He nodded.

"Maybe . . ."

"No," Jamie warned as she leaned closer, a gloved hand exploring. "I don't think we should touch it."

He watched Emma scrutinise the doors closely, her good eyesight making a detailed survey of the paintwork, trying to capture evidence of a trick in the doors' design.

"Careful," he told her.

When he glanced down the hallway, he was surprised to see the maid closing the apartment door. He hadn't heard her move out from the room behind them. As he watched, she did the act soundlessly. She shifted, losing colour, as if she were in an old black and white two-reeler. Jamie tried to catch her eye as she turned around but she didn't have anything he'd recognise as eyes. Where pupils and irises should be, there were only scorpions' tails, complete with stingers, waving in front of her.

He managed not to scream. In the grip of such torrential fear he found he could not move at all.

Thankfully, Emma's attention was firmly on the double doors, and she didn't notice the maid walking toward them. This time, the slippers the maid wore created barely a sound as they whisked her over the carpet, and her legs, which wore stockings under her black skirt, were as silent as a cat's. As she came, her scorpion tail eyes waved from side to side beneath her eyelashes. She turned at the last, when she was barely a foot from them, like an insect marching along a pre-determined track.

Jamie expelled a sigh of relief as the kitchen door closed behind her. Watching her had made him dizzy, as if he were viewing the world from behind trick-lensed eyeglasses: again, she'd moved like a clunky machine, as if a part of her was taking moments to pass through other dimensions as she'd come toward them.

"What?" Emma asked, steering a quizzical look at him. She hadn't seen any of that but now she noticed his fright.

He shook his head as his eyes came back into regular focus. Because he had seen something else now, a swaying that rippled through the twin doors before them, drifting like curtains in a breeze on the eggshell paintwork.

"What?" Emma said again. "Jamie. Tell me."

"There," he said. She didn't need to know about the maid, or those eyes. Besides, his attention was somewhere else altogether now. He squinted. "I think I see . . ."

Finding a measure of determination within himself he didn't know existed, Jamie gripped Emma's hand and tightened his fist around the wicker basket that was not a wicker basket, and stepped toward the doors.

"Oh-my-gosh," he heard Emma say as she was dragged after him, oozing through the illusion of wood and paint, and they went right the way through to the other side.

Jamie gasped, swallowed his breath.

They were stood in a square of light. Shading his eyes to look byond it, Jamie saw they were in a large, chilly hanger. It looked like the sort of enormous space in which you might expect to find a zeppelin being constructed, with astonishingly high ceilings held up by a tangled network of struts and crossbeams that were only faintly visible. The floor beneath them was concrete, and in places dried patches of what might have been oil spread out in stains. The illumination came from strip-lighting hanging from strung chains, with rope-twist electrical cables sagging between them. Jamie thought of pool halls, careful oblongs of light over blue baize. Within the thick dark corridors between the lights shadows of unlikely sizes seemed to sway and stutter with uneasy intent. When Jamie turned around, swinging the basket in one hand, steering Emma with the other, there was no sign of the doorway they'd just stepped through, only walls of sheet metal a little way from them.

"How do we get back?" Emma said.

"I don't know." He didn't have the impression of a curtain, a thin veil between realities, as he'd suddenly noticed back in apartment 337's hallway. "I don't know."

"Hello," a voice called from somewhere deep within the hanger. "Hell-lo-o."

The speaker sounded like a man trying to sing while being strangled. The syllables hung as an echo before fading to maddening inaudibility at the edge of their hearing. Jamie and Emma looked for the speaker somewhere in the tablets of visible, lighted space.

"Who is that?" Emma asked Jamie, knowing he had no more idea than she did.

"Someone over there, I think," Jamie said, believing he might have caught the sound of something shuffling determinedly in the thickly dark corridors between the lights. "Come on, away from the wall." They moved from one brilliant square of light, passing through darkness, and then into another. In the blind straights – which were about ten feet of pure deep darkness each – the temperature dipped by noticeable degrees. They moved from island light to island light, cautiously aware of presences they could not see and thankfully did not encounter in the spells away from the illumination, though the suspected presence of these creatures seemed to herd them toward the centre of the open space of what Jamie had come to think of as the hanger.

Then the strips nearest the walls were doused, and oblongs of light blinked out one after another, forcing them to steer into the middle of the hanger, leaving them in the one remaining inner area of brightness. Jamie couldn't shake the feeling of being corralled like livestock into a pen.

"Oh no," Emma whispered.

"Shh," Jamie said anxiously and moved them away from from where the darkness pressed the edges of the light, and where he was now sure unseen masses were pressing as close as they dared without revealing themselves.

In the distance, though it was impossible to tell how far away it was exactly, a flame flared into life with a sudden thrashing of sound. It grew in brilliance and size, approaching. Whoever held it, they carried it at arm's length. As it bobbed toward them, taking more time than seemed reasonable to make the progress it was making (the hanger couldn't be that big, could it?), all Jamie could see of the hand holding it was that its fingers were oversized and wearing large white rubber gloves. He couldn't be certain of exactly how many fingers there were on that hand either, but the tally wasn't good.

"I don't like this," Emma told him, voice fearful breath.

Pulling her closer into his embrace, Jamie was too busy squinting at the figure and trying to make his maths work in relation to those fingers to reply. A grim fascination needed satisfying as to the nature of the person behind the flame. The flickering torchlight made a pattern of an absurd face, but then the orange flame crossed in front of the speaker (surely this had to be the person who'd greeted them earlier, the owner of the strangled voice) and it was impossible to make out any more of him. A checked shirt perhaps, maybe braces, a too pale dome of a head. Who could say?

"Hello," Jamie called. He narrowed his eyes further on the chance he might see more. "Who's there?"

"Jamie," Emma warned. But it was too late. He'd let his voice out.

"Come on, tell us. Who is that?" he asked into the darkness.

His words felt so small in the hanger, thin and metallic. They hardly seemed capable of advancing on the air before weakening and becoming lost and shrunken by the dark.

"Put down the Grimaldiwick," the strangled voice instructed from behind the flame. "At the edge of the light."

"The Grimaldi . . . ?"

"It means the basket," Emma hissed, and somehow Jamie knew she was right and that this had to be the true name of the thing. The Grimaldiwick.

He complied, placing it at the edge, careful that he himself should remain within the illumination of the strip-bulb overhead. The electricity was buzzing through the tube, and it felt as fragile as a fluttering moth. Please don't let it fail, Jamie prayed. He slid his hand down his trousers, to palm away the greasy and slick memory his flesh had of being in contact with the basket, wondering what would come next.

The answer was that he and Emma jumped as Glenn Miller began to play. "Moonlight Serenade."

The strangled voice spoke above the mellow tone of the old music. "Thank you, Mister Purcell, for responding to our request to attend tonight. And your good lady wife also."

"I really don't like this," Emma told Jamie quietly. Neither did he. He felt himself tensing, the awareness of a hundred eyes – or perhaps scorpion tails – in the darkness following his every twitch and facial expression. He couldn't find words to reassure Emma.

"And for fetching," the voice said, "the Grimaldiwick. For that we are truly grateful. It has been lost for a long, long time. "

As if in response to the clown's strangled tones, the basket began to glow. A garish yellow light oozed from its form, swelling and then waning as the music sang out. From somewhere in the darkness of the hanger large motors began to turn, coughing to life, and a brisk wind picked up, the spinning hum of rotors. "There's machinery in here," Jamie said incredulously, but failed to locate it, no matter how intently he scanned the surrounding void. Not a glint of light shone from any metal carapace. He had seen no clue that there was anything large enough to produce the machine noises earlier, when the other lights had been working.

Emma's fingers dug into his arm.

"Look, the whatever it is, the *thing* with the torch, it's coming," she told him.

Jamie tugged her to one side protectively, always

making sure to stay within the brightest influence of the light. For some reason he felt there was safety within its touch, that whatever strange horde stood shuffling within the dark would not step out into visibility, perhaps if only to protect their fellows from their own grim apparitions. Now the bearer of the flame was approaching the couple again.

"Please say it's after the basket and not us," Emma said.

"Yes. I think so." But he couldn't know for sure.

Jamie watched fascinated, in anticipation of a great dread as the creature who'd spoken came into view. The sound of the machinery remained at a steady clattering hum, so he didn't hear the lope that accompanied the shuffling oversized feet.

A pale and worn clown, with a tonsure of orange hair and a bulbous ar-oogha horn nose, stepped from the shadows into the slight illumination beyond the edge of the light. As it did so the Zippo lighter that the massive flame grew from clicked out. The clown had an exploded cigar stapled to one corner of his lips. His mouth was painted in a sad magenta smile. Vicious strangulation wounds twisted around his too long neck, a neck that had been stretched and narrowed by a noose, Jamie thought, or something equally as hideous. Suspenders from the shoulders of a checked shirt maintained a pair of wide, hoop-belted trousers that led down to a pair of oversized boots. One of the clown's gloved hands was missing, and the stumpy arm protruding from beneath the cloth of the checked shirt showed mangled flesh that had been bound shut with big, bright red stitches tied in an extravagant bow.

But not tightly enough. Blood, dark and slow, oozed and dripped from fissures that had not been sealed sufficiently to do the job of repairing the wound.

"Oh my God," Jamie murmured.

The clown showed them his sad smile and the swaying scorpion tails where the pupils of his eyes should be, then advanced to the thing he had called the Grimaldiwick.

As he extended his remaining hand into the light, smoke rose from his exposed flesh, hissing and curling like a scared cat's arched back. His skin began to moulder and stray wisps of flame lifted from the arm visible between the cartoonish glove and the sleeve of his shirt. The light was burning it. But the clown seemed not to care and didn't reveal any discomfort.

Jamie silenced Emma's cry by smothering her mouth with his palm. He held her close, in a hug. Felt her trembling. Or perhaps he was the one who was trembling, he really couldn't have said.

The basket still glowed, it still broadcast music, the machinery in the dark maintained its heavy hum and clatter, a whir of wind growing as the clown attended to the basket. To Jamie's and Emma's eyes – which admittedly might not be the best for seeing with in this strange place, and therefore may have failed to grasp the more subtle nuances that scorpion tails might detect – the Grimaldiwick continued to resemble the unassuming wicker basket they had taken it for when they'd first encountered it.

"Thank you for returning our beloved," the clown said at last, exercising its ruined vocal chords once more as its face smoked greyly in the light. And then, weeping spots of blood, he shuffled back into the darkness, leaving the aroma of singed flesh in the air, while dragging the glowing basket after him. As the clown went deeper into the folded dark, the basket's eerie and uncomfortable light made butter forms of creatures too large and too thin, too fat and too bulbous, too swollen and too necrotic to have existed outside of the fiercest of nightmares. They swarmed around the glow and then backed off, moving like a shoal of diseased fish into the deeper, lightless vault of the hanger. Jamie thought he heard great, leather wings unfold and spread, then beat upon the air to lift creatures he'd rather not see or imagine into the dark. All the same, he pictured them swooping beneath the struts and crossbeams holding up the roof, despite trying to press such thoughts to the back of his mind.

"Is it over?" Emma whispered. He still held her to him. She'd been crying. The silver tracks of her tears were visible on her cheeks. "What about us? Can we go?"

"I don't know."

The clown had come to a stop, was dimly visible a way off from them. He waited until the basket had stopped producing music, and then sank to his knees before it as the glow also faded. Only darkness hung outside the safe oblong of light Jamie and Emma stood within. Long moments of silence passed as the machinery switched off and the breeze abandoned the hanger. Jamie's ears sang with tinnitus, but even beyond the high sibilant ringing he couldn't hear the whine of airborne creatures whirling around the high dark, no matter how much he strained to do so.

And then the basket began to glow again, a sickly green glow like the water in an aquarium takes on when it hasn't been cleaned for a long time.

For some reason he was never to explain, even many years later, when this experience seemed like the weirdest of dreams and nothing that he could ever persuade himself to believe was real, Jamie was struck by the sudden notion that he and Emma were attending a religious service. The basket had produced a hymn of sorts, the glow was a weird ceremonial communication, and now, with the initial benediction over, something else was about to happen.

What did come next was that a hideous choir of the congregation, still hidden in the shadows, produced the most unutterably terrible sound that Jamie Purcell had ever heard in his forty-three years on earth. Though he would live well into his eighties, there was not a single thing in the whole of the rest of his life that would compare to that dirge. Not the sound of Emma's dying breath, the collapse of the World Trade Center, or the rumble of the earthquake that hit Kobe. And whenever he looked up into the warmth of the summer night and saw the display of the immense universe and its celestial dance, when he thought of the massive silence between the stars, he experienced a feeling of thankful prayer that there was not air enough to carry sound between the blazing suns, that this bleak and unforgiving hymn could not pass between worlds.

As the choir of discontents and malformed monsters continued, the one-armed clown picked up the basket and carried it deeper into the darkness, taking the worshippers with him.

Somewhere a gong rang. Somewhere a thousand voices screamed. Somewhere the pitiful lamented the loss of the furnace and wailed for a return to Hell. And Jamie and Emma Purcell attended this church of warped comedies, knowing they could not leave until the ceremony was over and the congregation's hapless laughter had dissolved to less than the whisper of giggles in the chill, darkening air, as finally the light above them went out.

Closing Credits

The following tales first appeared, in slightly different form, in the following: "What I Wouldn't Give" on Amazon Kindle; "Tied Up Good and True," "Lies We Tell the Trojans," and "All That Remains of Silence" in *Supernatural Tales*, edited by David Longhorn. My love and thanks to all who helped in the construction of this book and making the tales better: and especially to Michelle, who did so much, as ever.

MPL - Sept 2018

36797367R00144

Printed in Great Britain
by Amazon